P9-EML-979

TOES

ALSO BY TOR SEIDLER

THE DULCIMER BOY

TERPIN

A RAT'S TALE

THE TAR PIT

THE WAINSCOTT WEASEL

MEAN MARGARET

THE SILENT SPILLBILLS

THE REVENGE OF RANDAL REESE-RAT

BROTHERS BELOW ZERO

BRAINBOY AND THE DEATHMASTER

TOR SEIDLER

TOES

Illustrations by Eric Beddows

LAURA GERINGER BOOKS
An Imprint of HarperCollins*Publishers*

Toes

 Printed in the United States of America. For information address HarperCollins Children's Books, a division of HarperCollins Publishers, 1350 Avenue of the Americas, New York, NY 10019.
www.harperchildrens.com

Library of Congress Cataloging-in-Publication Data
Seidler, Tor.
Toes / Tor Seidler ; illustrations by Eric Beddows.— 1st ed.
p. cm.
Summary: After getting lost on Halloween night when he is only a few months old, an intelligent seven-toed kitten makes his way into the life of a struggling musician.
ISBN 0-06-054099-0 — ISBN 0-06-054100-8 (lib. bdg.)
[1. Cats—Fiction. 2. Musicians—Fiction.] I. Beddows, Eric, date, ill. II. Title.
PZ7.S45526To 2004
[Fic]—dc22 2003014173
CIP
AC

Typography by Alicia Mikles
1 2 3 4 5 6 7 8 9 10

First Edition

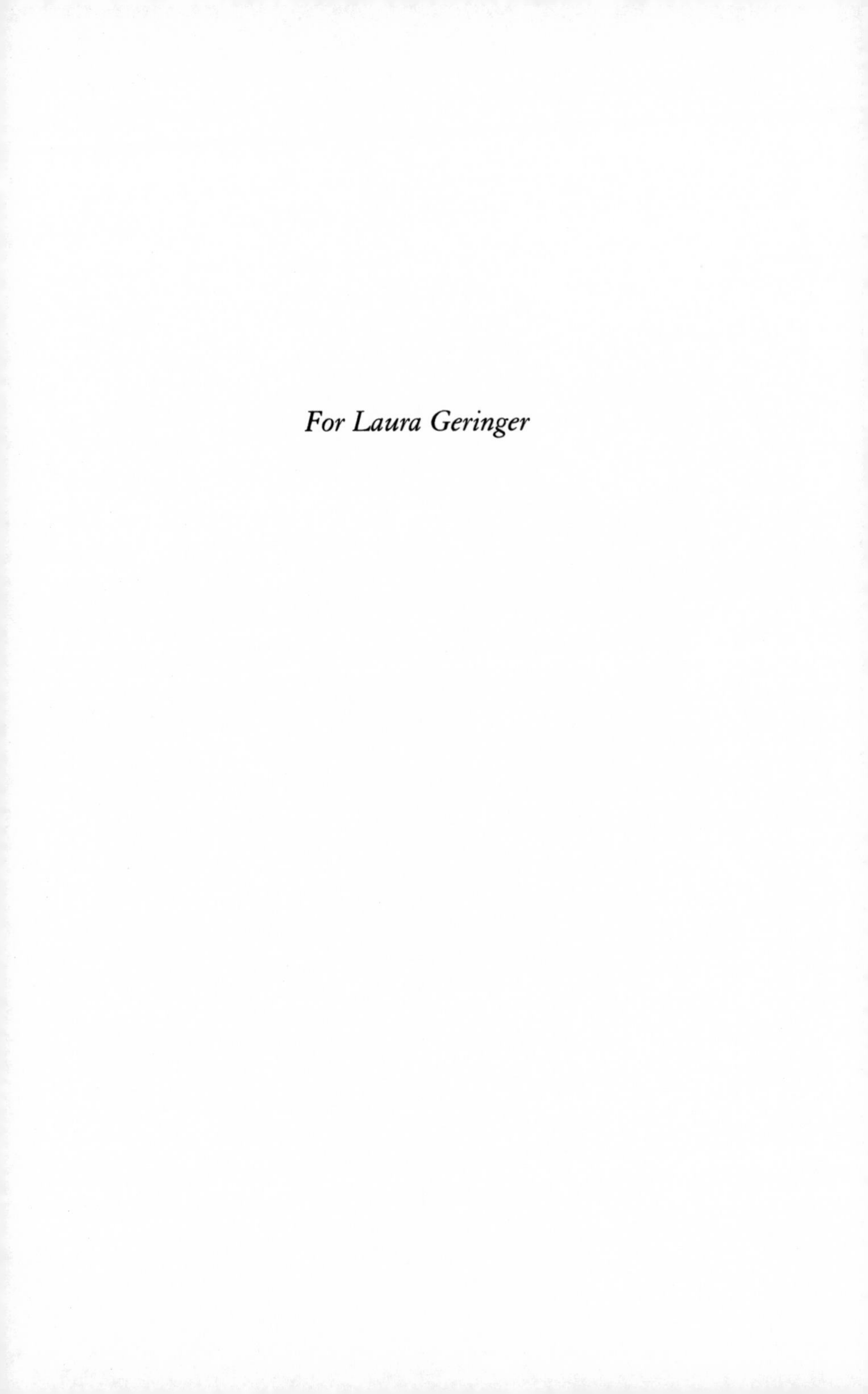

For Laura Geringer

TOES

1

"Where are they?" chimed Melissa and Tucker, jostling into the house behind their parents.

"Well," Mr. McDonahue said, "Fatima's been nursing them behind the hot-water heater."

Mrs. McDonahue said, "Take your bags up first, please," but Mr. McDonahue's voice apparently penetrated better, for the two kids dropped their suitcases and hurtled toward the kitchen. John, their older brother, was dying to do likewise. As of tomorrow, however, he would be a sophomore in high school, which seemed a little old for getting gushy over a bunch of kittens. Luckily, his parents exchanged a smile and traipsed after the younger kids, giving John the all-clear to dump his bag and follow.

In the sunlit kitchen Tucker already had a fur ball in either hand—one black with white stockings, the other nearly pure white—while Melissa had a pure-black one. John ducked into the utility room and emerged with one that was mottled black and white.

"They're so cute," Melissa cooed, stroking hers. "Have you named them yet?"

"We waited for you," Mrs. McDonahue said.

"Fact is," Mr. McDonahue said, "we've hardly seen hide nor hair of them."

"We can keep them, right?" Tucker pleaded.

"Please," Melissa said.

"I suppose, if everybody helps out," Mrs. McDonahue said.

"Yes!" cried Tucker.

"That one's got to be Socks," John said, pointing at the white-stockinged kitten.

"Yours looks like a Melissa," Tucker told his brother.

"No way," said the human Melissa.

"How about Labor Day then? Seeing as it's Labor Day."

"That's not a cat name," Melissa said contemptuously. "Besides, they were born right after we left for camp, right?"

"August fifth," Mrs. McDonahue said. "How about Spots?"

"Socks and Spots," Tucker said, grinning.

"That white one looks like a Fergie," Melissa said.

John checked the kitten in question and pronounced it a boy.

"Ferdinand then," Melissa said. "And this one's . . . eeek!"

Melissa dropped the black kitten onto the linoleum floor.

"What is it, sweetie?" Mrs. McDonahue asked.

"His paws!"

Mr. McDonahue picked up the stunned kitten.

"I'll be darned. We had cats on the farm with six toes, but this little guy's got seven!"

"Really?" said John, trading kittens with his father. "Wow! Seven on every paw."

"Guess he'll have to be Toes," Mrs. McDonahue said.

"Once our science club starts meeting," John said, "can I take him to show Dr. Medlicott?"

"I don't see why not," Mrs. McDonahue said. "But where's Fatima? She hasn't let them wander two feet away from her for a month."

Melissa opened the back door, which had a little cat door in the bottom, and called out into the fenced-in backyard: "Fattie, we're home!"

But Fatima didn't come.

"Maybe she got stuck up in that tree again," Melissa said, stepping out onto the patio.

It was a cool afternoon but fairly warm in the sun. However, Fatima wasn't sunning herself on her favorite flagstone. Nor was she up in the maple tree. Rejoining the others in the kitchen, Melissa speculated that Fatima might be off sulking, jealous of all the attention the kittens were getting.

"I doubt that," Mrs. McDonahue said. "Now, seriously, kids, take your things up to your rooms."

She and Mr. McDonahue, who'd gotten up early to drive to Camp Rokokoma, soon went upstairs to their own room.

"There you are, Fattie," Mrs. McDonahue said, seeing Fatima curled up on the foot of their bed.

But Fatima didn't raise her head. Mrs. McDonahue went over and stroked her.

"Good God," she whispered.

"What is it?" Mr. McDonahue said.

"She's cold as a stone."

"What?"

Mr. McDonahue came over and felt the cat. "My God. She was fine this morning."

"I don't understand it," Mrs. McDonahue said, tears springing into her eyes. "She was only five years old."

"Poor gal."

Mrs. McDonahue yanked a tissue from the box on the night table and blew her nose. "You know, her mother died young. Remember the funny little man at the animal shelter? With the pink-tinted glasses?"

"That's right. Weak heart, he said."

While Mrs. McDonahue pulled out a second tissue to dab her eyes, Mr. McDonahue gave his a quick wipe with his sleeve.

"It's amazing, when you think about it," Mrs. McDonahue said. "She lasted just long enough so the kittens could get along without her."

"She was a trouper. I bet she came up here so they wouldn't have to see her this way."

"Maybe the kids shouldn't either. We could pretend she ran away."

But Mr. McDonahue had grown up on a farm, where you learned early on that death is part of life—a lesson city kids like theirs often missed out on.

Of course, there were tears. Melissa, whose bed Fatima had favored, was particularly distraught. So as soon as possible Mrs. McDonahue shepherded everyone back down to the kitchen and the more cheerful sight of the kittens.

"Does this mean these cuties will die young, too?" Melissa said, scooping Socks up off the kitchen floor.

"They probably have defective genes," John said gloomily.

"Defective or not, they look mighty hungry," Mr. McDonahue said. "Would the pet store be open on Labor Day?"

"The whole mall's open," said Mrs. McDonahue.

Soon after she and Mr. McDonahue had taken off for Camp Rokokoma that morning, Fatima had informed her kittens that she, too, was setting off on a journey. But that didn't keep the kittens from starting to meow for her now. They were still at it when Mr. McDonahue returned from the pet store, and they quieted down only when bowls of warm formula and wet food appeared on a piece of newspaper in a corner of the kitchen.

Till now the kittens had only sucked milk out of their mother, but it didn't take them long to master this new way of eating. After their first solid meal they started yawning and tottered off into the dim utility room. As they made their way toward the hot-water heater, they spotted something new in the corner farthest from the litter box and veered that way. Along with the food and formula, Mr. McDonahue had bought them a wicker basket with a nice blue cushion in it, figuring the least he could do was provide the poor motherless creatures with a warm bed. But before Toes could reach it, someone scooped him up.

While John was reexamining the twenty-eight-toed curiosity, Melissa and her mother wrapped Fatima in a pillowcase and laid her out in a gift box from Saks Fifth Avenue. The burial, at the end of the backyard, was attended by the whole family. Tucker dug a hole between two azalea bushes. Melissa had the honor of placing the makeshift casket into it. Mrs. McDonahue then lifted the lid, stuck in Fatima's favorite toy—a chewed-up fur mouse that had once had a bell around its neck—and put the lid back on. After John filled in the grave, Mr. McDonahue drove a white stake into the soft earth. On it he'd etched FATIMA and the years of her birth and death with a black pen.

As the bereaved family shuffled back toward the house, Melissa pointed at her older brother.

"Mom, look!"

"Really, John," Mrs. McDonahue said, noticing the little black-furred head poking out of his jacket pocket. "They're only a month old. They need their sleep."

When John deposited Toes back in the utility room, the kitten headed instinctively for the litter box. He was still a little woozy from his earlier fall onto kitchen floor, but he managed to scale the box's side. After doing his business and neatly burying it, he climbed out and made his wobbly way toward his siblings, who were curled up in the inviting new bed.

Stopping short of it, Toes cleared his throat. "Mother's in a fancy box," he said solemnly. "They gave her a mouse before they filled in the hole."

The other three kittens lifted their heads.

"Huh?" Spots said.

"They buried Mother in the backyard," Toes said.

"Baloney," said Ferdinand.

"She had to go away on a journey," said Socks. "Remember?"

"I saw her in the box," Toes said. "Now she's underground."

"Liar," Socks said.

"I just saw."

"How come?"

"How come what?"

"How come you saw and we didn't?"

"He's trying to be a big shot," Ferdinand said.

"No, I'm not," Toes said. "I think one of them's interested in my paws."

"Must like freaks," Spots said, nudging Socks.

Socks snickered, and so did Ferdinand. Toes mustered a weak smile. They'd all gotten along so well for the first couple of weeks of their lives, when they'd been cuddled together, warm and blind, dividing their time between sleeping and being fed and licked by their mother. But once their eyes opened, things had changed. Though their mother had insisted that a few extra toes meant nothing, Toes's siblings had begun to spurn him.

Toes had figured the tragic news would end all that. He'd figured they would cling to each other now that they had no mother. But the others seemed even less friendly than before. So Toes just climbed onto the blue cushion and curled up.

"Come on," Spots complained. "Not so close."

Toes shifted over toward Ferdinand.

"You think I want an alien next to me?" Ferdinand said, making a face. "It's probably contagious."

Socks wasn't much more cordial, calling him the Cat from Mars, so Toes slid off the cushion onto the chilly linoleum and sniffed his way to the familiar spot behind the hot-water heater. The floor there was warmer and retained a hint of their mother's smell. He wished she could come back to lick him. But he knew she couldn't, so he licked the crumbs of litter off his front paws himself. Once they were clean, he studied them forlornly. There was no getting around the fact that they were bigger than any of his siblings', plainly misshapen. But could they really be contagious?

Next morning, Tucker and Melissa burst into the utility room and grabbed three kittens out of the basket.

"Where's the other guy?" Tucker said.

Melissa found Toes curled up behind the hot-water heater. "Aren't you the exclusive one," she said, picking him up.

They set the kittens on the Persian rug in the living room, and Melissa pulled a ball of yarn from her mother's knitting basket. Soon she was screeching with delight at the sight of the kittens rolling around with it. Tucker dangled a length of yarn just over their heads, jerking it out of reach whenever they took a swipe. The only one who succeeded in snagging it was Toes, who had seven little razor-sharp toenails per paw instead of just five.

Both Mr. and Mrs. McDonahue worked, and that day was the kids' first day of school, so the kittens were soon left to their own devices. They started batting the ball of yarn around, treating the Persian rug as a soccer field, the legs of two end tables as goalposts. Thanks to his bigger paws, Toes excelled at this, too, and when he suggested choosing up sides for a game, Spots actually agreed to team up with him. Toes went all out and scored the first two goals. When Ferdinand made the next one, Socks ran up and rubbed whiskers with him, so when Spots scored next, Toes did the same thing.

"Don't!" Spots shrieked, jumping back.

"What's the matter?" Toes asked.

"I don't want to catch it," Spots said.

"But I'm sure my toes aren't contagious."

"How do you know?"

"Just because he scored two goals," Socks said, "he thinks he knows everything."

"More toes, more brains," Ferdinand said, smirking.

Toes slunk off into the dining room. For a while he diverted himself by winding among the forest of chair and table legs there, but the wood floor was cold, so he eventually moved on to the kitchen. After a snack—the bowls on the newspaper still had some food and milk in them—he wandered into a front hall with a mountainous staircase off to one side. He was naturally curious where it led, but the stairs were too tall and slick to climb, so he moved on into a cozy room with wall-to-wall carpeting. To his right was a comfortable-looking leather armchair, but the sofa, off to his left, looked easier to climb, thanks to a skirt around the bottom. By putting all twenty-eight toenails to good use, he managed to claw his way up onto the cushions. From there he had a panoramic view across a coffee table strewn with glossy magazines to a big console with a dark-glass window that gave back a slightly distorted reflection of the room. Unfortunately, he didn't have the sofa kingdom to himself. Someone else was perched on the farther cushion: someone as black as he was, and about the same length, but furless. Scrunching low, Toes stalked. His competition gave off no scent and clearly wasn't scared, refusing to budge an inch. Working up his courage, Toes leaped forward and gave him a quick swat. He didn't swat back. Feeling bolder, Toes pounced on top of him, grabbing him with all twenty-eight toes. His adversary didn't put up the slightest resistance. Toes licked him. He didn't taste very good. But even so Toes dragged him triumphantly into a corner of the sofa and started giving him little nips and swats to make sure he understood who was boss. After a while Toes flipped him onto his back. His front was covered with all sorts of funny nubs and buttons.

While toying with his victim, Toes heard a human voice and dove behind a needlepoint cushion. Would he get in trouble for being up on the sofa? He peered cautiously around the cushion's edge. There wasn't a McDonahue in sight. But another human being, a stranger with no hair and thick eyeglasses, had appeared in the window to the console. The man seemed to be talking to *him*—he was looking Toes squarely in the eye—but of course Toes couldn't understand human speech. Then the bald man vanished and a wondrous sight took his place: a flock of tiny pink birds flying over a shimmering lake. Toes's heart raced. If only he could grab one of the birds and see how it tasted! But the birds were flying around inside the console—and soon *they* disappeared, too, replaced by a herd of tiny horned animals raising dust as they sped across an open field.

The magic window revealed wonder after wonder. Human beings talking, cars screeching, fish jumping out of the water, human beings firing guns, airplanes taking off, human beings drinking soft drinks, human beings throwing balls, human beings riding horses, human beings kissing each other. Most of these things were utter mysteries to Toes, but the spectacle was still mesmerizing, especially when a human being poured something into a bowl and set the bowl on the floor. A whole family of cats crowded around it! The cats all looked perfect—five toes on every paw—and none of them replied to Toes's meowing overtures. But he still enjoyed their company.

Riveting as the magic window was, Toes was only a month old, and eventually he dozed off. The sound of a door closing woke him. As he blinked at a woman holding up a box of laundry soap inside the console, familiar voices mingled with hers.

"For goodness' sake!" Mrs. McDonahue said, appearing in the doorway. "Who left the TV on?"

"Not me!" Tucker cried, materializing at her side.

"Don't look at me," Melissa said in the background.

Hiding behind the needlepoint cushion, Toes peeked out as Mrs. McDonahue leaned down and picked up his vanquished foe. She gave him a poke, and the magic window went dark.

"John was probably watching that science

show before he caught his bus," she murmured, dropping Toes's adversary onto a pile of magazines. "Better feed the kitties."

Soon after she left the room, Toes got a wonderful whiff of heating milk. But climbing down from the sofa proved to be more of a challenge than climbing up. He tried the headfirst approach and nearly fell. Then he turned and tried climbing down backward. He made it halfway before losing his grip.

But this tumble wasn't nearly as painful as yesterday's. Somehow he managed to land on his feet—and the carpet was considerably softer than linoleum.

In the kitchen his siblings had started dinner without him. Spots was lapping up warm formula from one bowl, while Socks and Ferdinand were gobbling wet food from the other. When Toes joined Spots, Spots padded off to the food bowl. When Toes went to get some food, the others all switched to the milk.

That night Toes didn't bother trying to join them on the fancy bed, going straight to his place behind the hot-water heater. And the next morning he didn't bother trying to play yarn soccer with them, heading instead for the cozy room, where he again scaled the sofa. Once more, his adversary was already staking a claim to the high country, and once more, Toes easily subdued him. In fact, he was so lifeless that Toes decided he wasn't an adversary at all, just some kind of mechanical gizmo. Today, however, the interesting beings inside the console kept a dark curtain over their window. Toes stared and stared, wishing they would show themselves, but they refused. Were they asleep? Or had Mrs. McDonahue scared them away by poking the gizmo? Toes started poking the gizmo himself. After jabbing several of the buttons, he hit one in the corner. Presto! the curtain lifted. There, to Toes's delight, was a cat. Not a real cat. A cartoon cat, even funnier-looking than he was.

All of a sudden the cartoon cat's back arched, and his eyes grew to saucers. A big cartoon dog joined him in the window. Toes cowered back behind the needlepoint cushion—till he heard human voices and peeked out. There wasn't a human being in sight: only the cartoon cat and the cartoon dog, carrying on a conversation in human speech.

Toes was dying to know what they were saying, but of course it all went right over his head. Even when human beings hogged the window away from the cartoon cat and dog, Toes kept his ears pricked, hoping to figure out their language in case the cat returned. But trying to make sense of nonsense was exhausting, and finally he couldn't keep his eyes open.

Again the sound of the front door woke him. Something told him the McDonahues might be unhappy if they found the magical window open again, so he pounced on the gizmo, hitting the button in the corner. The window went dark and silent.

After dinner that night, when the other three kittens crawled into bed, Toes padded off to his usual spot behind the hot-water heater. But he'd taken such a long nap that he really wasn't very sleepy, and after a while he tiptoed—on all twenty-eight toes—past his sleeping siblings and out the cracked-open door into the kitchen. Water was running there. Melissa was rinsing plates and sticking them into the dishwasher.

A different and far more wonderful sound lured Toes into the living room. Mr. McDonahue was reading a newspaper in an armchair; Mrs. McDonahue was in another chair with her knitting in her lap, a rapt expression on her face.

"Isn't this beautiful, honey?" she said.

Mr. McDonahue lowered his paper and put on a listening expression. "Mozart, is it?"

"Schubert, actually."

"It's very nice."

Mr. McDonahue devoted a few more seconds to listening, then returned to his paper. But Mrs. McDonahue didn't knit. She leaned her head against the chair back, smiling, and closed her eyes.

Toes crept under her chair and curled up there on the Persian rug. After a while he, too, closed his eyes, and the ravishing river of sound carried him off to a place where no one cared about trivial things like a few extra toes.

When Toes hit the corner button on the gizmo the next morning, the cartoon cat reappeared in the magic window. But he wasn't talking to a cartoon dog; he was talking to a cartoon mouse cowering in a mousehole. To Toes's dismay, even the mouth-watering mouse was using human speech!

Try as he might, Toes couldn't understand a word.

Toes's days began to fall into a routine. Weekdays he spent in the cozy room, peering in the magic window, trying his best to decipher the mysterious human language. On weekends, Mr. McDonahue often monopolized the cozy room, but he didn't seem to mind Toes joining him to watch cars going in circles around a racetrack or human beings running in circles around a diamond-shaped field. In the evening Toes liked to join Mrs. McDonahue in the living room to bask in the beautiful sounds.

One day, Mrs. McDonahue shut the kittens up in a small prison with a barred door. Socks and Spots and Ferdinand huddled together at one end of the cramped space, leaving the other end for Toes. As the prison started to sway back and forth, the three kittens in one end trembled violently. Toes was frightened, too, but he'd witnessed a scene in the magic window of a human being taking a cat on a train in a carrying case, so he wasn't totally panic-stricken. Through the bars he watched familiar household landmarks pass by; then they were outside, bombarded by all sorts of mysterious sights and smells—though Toes recognized the shimmering arc of water sprinkling the front yard from lawn-seed commercials. Suddenly they were back inside, by the easy chair in the cozy room. Or so the leather smell indicated. When the place began to vibrate and move, Toes realized they couldn't be in the cozy room after all. But while his cell mates let out strangled wails, Toes had seen enough cars in the magic window to realize they must be in one, and since the car didn't seem to be going round and round in circles, he felt fairly safe. The only times cars seemed to crash was when they were racing in circles on weekends.

The car made a left turn, then a right; then the vibrations ceased and Mrs. McDonahue carried the prison out of the car and into a place with the most confusing odors imaginable: all sorts of different animal smells mixed with a nose-prickling smell of cleanser. The prison came to rest on a table under a bright light. The door opened, and a hairy hand—definitely not Mrs. McDonahue's—reached in and grabbed a whimpering Ferdinand.

A few minutes later Ferdinand returned, quaking from head to tail, and Socks was whisked away.

"What do they do to you out there?" Spots squeaked.

"They torture you," Ferdinand said.

"How?" Spots cried.

"With needles and knives." Ferdinand groaned. "It's horrible!"

It was even more horrible for Toes. After he got fixed and had his shots, the hairy-handed veterinarian made him feel freakier than ever by carrying him all around the clinic, showing other human beings his paws. But there was one small consolation. By this time Toes had picked up the meaning of a few human words from the magic window—including the word for the magic window itself: TV—and today he learned a new one. Everyone who studied his paws exclaimed the same thing: "Seven!" So it stood to reason that this must be the number of his toes.

His theory was confirmed a few days later when John shut Toes up in the prison all by himself and carried him to his school, where Dr. Medlicott and the members of the science club all exclaimed:

"Wow, seven toes!"

After the kittens' second round of shots, several weeks later, they got a reward: collars with little brass tags that had their names and birth dates engraved on them. Soon the kittens were big enough to climb stairs and poke through the flap in the back door. At first they were skittish about venturing very far into the fenced-in backyard, among so many unfamiliar smells. What's more, the weather had turned colder. But there were still days when the sun felt wonderful on their fur, and out on the lawn there were insects to toy with and eat, and flies to bat out of the air, and falling leaves and birds and butterflies to chase. Toes, with his extra claws, had the most success at fly catching. He got no credit from his siblings, of course—but he got the flies themselves, which were a lot tastier than cat food.

One day, Toes chased an orange-and-black butterfly all the way to the fence at the back of the property. While he was looking up, swatting at the infuriating creature, his snout bumped against a white stake.

That evening, curled up underneath Mrs. McDonahue's chair listening to the beautiful sounds, Toes closed his eyes and felt his mother's warm, scratchy tongue on his fur and heard her warm, reassuring voice: "Don't worry about a few extra toes, honey. They don't mean a thing."

It was hard to know if Spots and Socks and Ferdinand disliked him because of his spare toes or resented him for being best at fly catching and yarn snagging and chair climbing—or for destroying the pretty illusion of their mother going on a journey. Whatever their reasons, they continued to give him the cold shoulder. So Toes continued to spend his days watching the magic window in the cozy room, his nights curled up alone behind the hot-water heater.

One Sunday morning the kittens all woke to a glorious new smell. Skipping their usual stretching, they pattered out into the kitchen, where John gave each of them a tiny fish-flavored treat that tasted ten times better than kitty chow—better even than fresh flies.

John soon gathered the whole household,

feline and human, in the living room. It was Halloween, and his brother and sister had spent the day before slaving over their costumes. But John, who felt he was getting a little old for trick-or-treating, had worked on something else.

"What the heck is that?" Tucker asked, pointing at a contraption on the coffee table.

"I call it the McDonahue box," John said.

"What's it for?" Melissa asked.

"Testing the intelligence of cats."

"Huh?" Tucker said.

As soon as John set the thing on the rug, all four kittens crowded around it. It gave off an irresistible smell of fish treat.

"Okay, guys, I'm only going to show you this once," John said. "To open the door, you pull down this little lever like so."

John pulled a lever on the outside of the box, and the door popped open. The kittens all tried to rush in, but John closed the door before any of them could.

"What on earth did you put in there, sweetie?" Mrs. McDonahue asked.

"It's a fish treat laced with a little catnip," John said. "It's supposed to drive them wild."

It did. Socks and Spots and Ferdinand raced around the box sniffing like mad. Toes was intensely attracted to it as well, but they kept pushing him away, so he hung back.

"I'm afraid cats don't have that kind of intelligence, John," Mrs. McDonahue said. "They're not like dolphins, or chimpanzees. Their brains are very small. For them everything's instinct."

"But Mom, Spots is the smartest kitty in the world!" Melissa protested. "Aren't you, Spotsie?"

"Ferd's twice as smart," Tucker said.

"I used to figure Socks was the pick of the litter," Mr. McDonahue said thoughtfully, "but I've come around to Toes. He likes NASCAR."

And indeed when the three other kittens got frustrated and backed away from the box, Toes stepped up and pulled the lever. The door popped open. He dove in and devoured the treat.

"Way to go, Toes!" John cried.

As Toes emerged from the box, he didn't

miss the daggers in the eyes of his siblings, but he couldn't help licking his lips. The treat was so scrumptious, he actually felt light-headed, as if he were floating.

"That's amazing," Mrs. McDonahue said. "But it had to be a fluke."

John went into the kitchen and returned with another treat, which he shut up in the McDonahue box. Again Toes hung back as the other three kittens attacked it.

"Look at him!" Melissa exclaimed. "He's just watching them."

"Maybe he is the smartest," Tucker said.

"He's like a batter waiting for his pitch," Mr. McDonahue said.

The truth was, the word "lever" was new to Toes. But he'd recently learned the word "pull," and by watching John, he'd put two and two together. After a few minutes, Spots and Socks and Ferdinand got tired of being tantalized and drifted away. Toes went up and pulled the lever and dove in.

"He's a cat genius!" John cried. "Wait'll I tell Dr. Medlicott!"

As he came out of the box, Toes refrained from licking his chops.

"That was no fluke, sweetie," Mr. McDonahue said. "Toes knew exactly what he was doing."

"You're the most amazing cat in the world!" Melissa said, scooping Toes up.

Everyone in the family crowded around to stroke Toes's belly and scratch his ears. He'd never been so coddled.

"You know, he always comes in when I have on my music," Mrs. McDonahue said. "I assumed it was just a coincidence, but do you suppose he might actually enjoy it?"

"*I'm* convinced he's a sports fan," Mr. McDonahue said. "Want to come watch a game with me, Toes?"

"I think his head's a little bigger than the others'," Tucker said. "He must have a bigger brain."

All day long the family made a fuss over him. Later in the afternoon, John set out the box again, and after the others got sick of the game, Toes again waltzed up and claimed the delectable prize. But this time he brought it out and set it on the rug.

"Look!" Melissa cried.

"You've got to see this, Dad!" Tucker cried.

Mr. McDonahue, who was watching a football game, came out and joined the others in the living room.

"What is it?"

"Toes got the treat again," Melissa said. "But this time he's sharing it."

However, Ferdinand turned his nose up.

"Not after it was in *your* mouth," he said.

"You're just trying to impress them," said Socks.

"Let's go, guys," said Spots, and the other two kittens followed him out of the living room.

Since they didn't want it, Toes gobbled up the treat.

"Tomorrow I'm taking you to school again, Toes," John declared. "Dr. Medlicott's not going to believe it."

In the basement John found a high chair that hadn't been used since Tucker was a three-year-old, and when the family sat down to their early Sunday dinner, Toes joined them, perched at the table like a king on his throne. John even cut up part of one of his lamb chops and gave it to Toes on a butter plate along with a dab of green jelly. Toes wasn't crazy about the jelly, but the tender bits of lamb were even tastier than the fish treat.

After this memorable meal, Mr. McDonahue did the cleanup while Tucker and Melissa bolted upstairs to put on their Halloween costumes. Mrs. McDonahue sat down in the living room with Toes in her lap, stroking his fur in time to something wonderful that she called Mendelssohn.

Toes had been in such demand all day that he'd missed his usual naps, so when the music ended, he headed straight for the utility room. He curled up behind the hot-water heater and fell into a deep sleep. But he had a dreadful nightmare. He dreamed he was being buried alive in his mother's grave! It was so grisly that, exhausted as he was, he forced himself awake.

His eyes wouldn't open. Something was

pressing against them, holding them shut. Something was pressing against his snout, too. He gagged, trying to breathe. All he got was a mouthful of dust. He really and truly was buried alive!

But not in dirt. The smell was much worse than that. He flailed desperately, scraping with all twenty-eight toes. His head surfaced. He blinked. There, grinning at him from beyond the walls of the litter box—which hadn't been cleaned out since morning—were his siblings.

"Like your new bed, egghead?" Ferdinand said.

"Taste as good as the fish treat?" Socks asked.

"P.U.," Spots said, stepping back as Toes clambered out.

"Jeez, you're really stinking the place up," Socks said.

"Go hang out with your human pals, why don't you?" Ferdinand suggested.

Toes did stink. And he could hardly lick himself clean. It would be too disgusting. All he could do was shake himself. The other three gave him a wide berth as he skulked out into the kitchen.

He could hear the TV in the cozy room but headed instead for the cat flap in the back door. He'd never been outdoors at night before, but his eyes adjusted easily to the dark. He hopped off the patio and started rolling around on the grass. This got him only so clean, however. Remembering the sprinkler in the front yard, he bounded over to the stockade fence and leaped onto it. It was over six feet tall, beyond the climbing ability of most kittens. But most kittens don't have twenty-eight claws.

Toes balanced for a few seconds on the fence top, then threw himself over the far side and made a soft landing in the next-door neighbor's compost heap. He skirted a tangled vegetable garden and pattered past a brick house. Rounding the end of the fence, he saw the McDonahues' mountainous SUV. He crawled under it into their front yard.

Not a sprinkler in sight. Instead, propped

up on the front doorstep, there was a huge, horrible, decapitated head breathing fire out of its gap-toothed mouth.

Toes sprinted off down the sidewalk in terror, not stopping till he reached the street corner. As he crouched there catching his breath in the puddle of light under a streetlamp, a pair of ghoulish monsters emerged from the darkness. One had an axe stuck in his bloody head. The other was only bones: a walking skeleton.

Looking neither left nor right, Toes dashed straight across the street. An earsplitting screech: a braking minivan, barely missing him. In a blind panic he darted up a driveway. But there, in the bay window of a house, was another grotesque orange head with a fire burning inside the skull.

Toes shot under a hedge and sprinted across a backyard. Unlike the McDonahues', this backyard hadn't been raked, and he came out into an alley with his soiled fur coated with leafy flakes. Why, oh why, had he ever ventured outside? If he'd just gone into the living room, someone would have seen his condition and cleaned him up.

The alley ended on a street that wasn't a bit familiar. Toes sniffed the chilly night air. No familiar smells.

But he made out something familiar across the street: the silhouette of the school building where he'd been shown off to John's science club. There were no human beings on the front steps at this hour, no flag on the flagpole, no bikes in the bike rack. But it was definitely the place.

Toes scooted across and crouched at the foot of the steps, trying to reconstruct which way they'd walked home. Though he wasn't absolutely sure, he had an idea it was to the right. As he headed that way, a bloodcurdling bark froze him in his tracks.

A gigantic German shepherd came plowing around the corner of the school building, pulling a night watchman by its leash. Toes took off for all he was worth in the other direction. On the next street corner he encountered another walking skeleton, this one accompanied by two figures all in black with peaked hats and broomsticks.

Toes lit out down a side street. It led to a broad avenue. As he hunched by a fireplug near the curb, gasping for breath, a pair of goblins approached, chattering away in human speech.

Off went Toes in the other direction.

Soon he was entirely lost, wandering around a neighborhood quite different from the McDonahues'. There were fewer front yards. The houses were closer together and interspersed with storefronts and occasional looming apartment buildings, some with more scary orange heads glowing in windows. Slinking along, Toes shuddered every time a truck or bus rumbled by on the avenue. Eventually he came to another alley and picked up the scent of a cat. The alley was dark and oily, but Toes started down it, hoping maybe he could ask directions.

A tomcat, three times Toes's size, jumped out from behind a steel drum and let out a menacing hiss.

Toes scampered back to the avenue and leaped right off the curb. As soon as he landed, he skidded to a stop, caught in headlights. The car rolled past: a kind highly familiar from TV, with a red light on the roof and human beings in uniforms inside. Hearing the tomcat hiss behind him, Toes darted across the empty lanes.

As he climbed onto the median strip, a drop of water hit him on the head, right between his ears. By the time he reached the far side of the avenue, the skies had opened. For a while he just stood on the curb basking in the rain, relieved to have his fur cleansed of litter and leaf flakes. But soon, thoroughly drenched, he started to shiver. The icy drops got so thick that he had to dive under a parked car.

The gutter there was fast becoming a river, forcing him to remount the curb. On the other side of the sidewalk was one of the tall, forbidding-looking buildings they called housing projects on TV. Wedged between it and another project was a small house with a one-car garage. The small house didn't have a decapitated orange head in the window, so Toes made a dash for it. The garage door was down, impossible to squeeze under. He scrambled onto the front porch. It was so shallow the rain slanted in, and the door had no cat flap. Maybe only back doors had them, Toes reasoned. He climbed down and, blinded by the downpour, nearly tumbled headlong into a window well. He jumped down into it and peered through a pane of drizzly glass into a basement. It was dim down there, but he could make out a hot-water heater much like the one at the McDonahues'. Unfortunately, the window was locked.

Shivering uncontrollably now, he scrambled out of the window well. A narrow passageway divided the house from the project next door. He scooted down it, dodging broken bottles and dented cans and discarded ballpoint pens and dead batteries and soggy cigarette butts and crumpled candy wrappers. Behind the house was a weedy little backyard area featuring a garbage can and a rusted table and chair. The back door had no cat flap either. But there was another window well, and when he peered down into this one, he saw that one of the two panes of glass was missing, replaced by a piece of Masonite. He hopped down and pushed the Masonite with all his might. But he was still only a kitten. It wouldn't give.

Toes was desperate. If he didn't find a warm, dry place quickly, he would shiver to death. Maybe if he waited by the doors to one of the housing projects, someone would come in or out and he could dash into the lobby. He climbed out of the window well and started picking his way back down the litter-choked passageway but stopped after a few yards. He grabbed an old ballpoint pen in his mouth and returned to the window well in the rear of the little house. Though his extra toes made him a freak, they also made him surprisingly dexterous, and he was able to use the pen as a crowbar, prying a corner of the Masonite. After a couple more drenching minutes, he managed to loosen it and squeeze inside, out of the chilling downpour.

4

It was worse than the time he was dropped onto the kitchen floor. Instead of falling four feet onto linoleum, he fell nearly eight feet onto concrete.

But he was still young enough to have rubbery bones. After a dazed minute, he rose shakily to his feet, did a couple of experimental stretches, and peered around him. In the faint light filtering down from the window wells he made out a furnace and a stool and a stack of boxes and an old wardrobe and a table and a door and a steep staircase. He limped over to the furnace. It was stone cold. He dragged his weary, battered body over to the hot-water heater. It wasn't as warm as the one in the McDonahues' utility room, but it was giving off a bit of heat. He curled up into a tight ball beside the tank and passed out.

When he woke up, a dusty beam of sunlight was slanting from the front window well to a drain in the middle of the basement floor. The sunlight had more of an afternoon quality than a morning quality, and Toes's fur was nice and dry, so he figured he must have slept a long, long time.

After giving himself a thorough tongue bath, he sized up his situation. The two little windows were beyond his high-jumping abilities, and the walls were too hard for his claws. He went over to the door, which was ajar, and pushed his way into a small bathroom. It had a toilet and sink but no way out. He made an exploratory excursion up the stairs. The door at the top was shut.

As he slouched back down the stairs, he realized what a birdbrained thing he had done. To get out of the rain, he'd thrown himself into a dungeon. He was warm and dry, but what good was that when he had no way to escape and nothing to eat?

He burped—and got a whiff of lamb chop. Was it really less than a day since he'd been gorging on fish treats and juicy tidbits of lamb? It seemed like a week.

He went over and sniffed the stack of boxes. No food smells. He managed to open one box and pulled out a couple of old shoes. The leather was too hard to chew. One of the wardrobe doors wasn't quite closed, but when he stood on his hind legs and pawed it open, a stinging smell burned his nostrils. He shut the wardrobe, then climbed up onto the stool and from there onto the table. It was covered with tools: various screwdrivers, needle-nose plyers, a hammer, a chisel, coffee cans full of screws and nails and tacks. But the closest things to food were jars of putty and carpenter's glue.

There was a small puddle in the back of the basement where rain had leaked in from the loosened piece of Masonite. He lapped the water up, then crouched nearby, staring up at the front window. After a while the pole of sunlight dissolved, and the sound of traffic out on the avenue grew louder. The hot-water heater purred. The only other sounds were occasional creaks from overhead and the growling of his empty stomach.

Eventually he detected a new sound: a faint scratching. His heartbeat doubled, but he didn't move a whisker. Out of a little hole in the baseboard under the stairs popped a mouse. It ventured in a zigzagging path toward where Toes was crouched, stopping to sniff this and that. When it got past the drain, Toes pounced.

Evidently he had the same natural skill at mouse catching as he had at yarn soccer. And the mouse tasted delicious—every bit as good as lamb chop. He ate till he was stuffed, then hid the leftovers behind one of the boxes for a later meal.

Tasty as it was, mouse was salty. But the puddle was gone. Toes ducked into the little bathroom and peered up at the sink. It was much like the sinks in the McDonahues' house, and though he'd never used one, he knew they were a water source. He hopped up onto the toilet seat—and nearly slipped into the bowl. There was water down there, but it didn't smell very good, so he continued on up to the sink and with one of his seven-toed paws managed to turn the faucet. Rusty water sluiced out of the tap. It soon cleared up, but he couldn't stretch his neck out quite far enough to catch any on his tongue, and the basin was too turbulent for jumping into. He climbed back down to the floor and returned to the tool table, where he knocked over one of the coffee cans, spilling dozens of eye screws. He stuck the empty coffee can onto his head like a stovepipe hat and made his way back to the sink. He doffed the hat. It landed right side up in the sink, directly under the tap. When the can was brimful, he cut the water off. By stretching out his neck he could now sip at his leisure.

Much as he hated to think of litter boxes, he soon needed one, and though another tour of the basement revealed nothing with loose dirt or sand in it, he knew what toilets were for from commercials he'd seen on daytime TV for toilet-bowl cleansers. Unfortunately, after using it he found he wasn't quite tall enough yet to reach the flush.

Curled up by the hot-water heater again, he soon got a tantalizing whiff of fish. He followed his nose to the top of the stairs and heard a familiar human voice. Peering through an inch-high, light-filled gap under the door, Toes saw the bottom of a door frame and, beyond that, the bottom third of a TV screen. The voice belonged to the TV man who described the important things that had happened in the world that day.

Soon the man's voice gave way to a woman singing a jingle, and a pair of dingy tennis shoes and khaki cuffs crossed Toes's field of vision. But he didn't even consider scratching the door or whimpering. He was an intruder—and he'd seen a frightening TV movie about a place where unwanted pets were taken called the Pound. However, he stayed put and watched the bottom part of the TV till the screen went dark. Then he crept downstairs, took a few sips from the coffee can, and fell asleep by the hot-water heater.

Squeaky voices woke him. Lifting his head, he watched four mice creep out from under the stairs. They headed his way but stopped in a splotch of moonlight near the drain. Not being hungry, Toes just listened.

"Don't you love being up in the middle of the night! When the moon's so big and round and bright!"

"Do you suppose it's really made of green cheese?"

"If it is, I wish it would catch cold and sneeze."

"Then storms would be cheese drops instead of just rain!"

"And finding a meal wouldn't be such a pain!"

It was common knowledge that mice were addicted to mindless rhymes, but the McDonahues' house was mouse-free, so this was the first time Toes had ever actually heard any. The silly creatures approached the hot-water heater and ducked into a hole in the baseboard only a few feet away from where he was crouched.

The next morning Toes woke completely recovered from his drenching and tumble. After stretching, he finished off yesterday's mouse, but it didn't taste quite as delicious today. Maybe mouse meat didn't keep well—or maybe it was the harebrained rhymes still echoing in his head.

The weather was fine again, so he settled at the foot of the pole of sunlight. As it warmed his fur, a nice, nutty smell filled his nostrils, and he drifted into a luxurious doze.

When he opened his eyes, the sunlight was gone. He peered around at his forlorn surroundings, and the cold of the stone floor seeped into him. Even now he didn't miss his siblings, but he missed the McDonahues and their house terribly. It was clear he could survive in this basement. But what was the point of surviving with nothing to live for?

As he crouched on the hard, chilly floor, a new sound drifted down from above. It was related to the sounds he used to listen to with

Mrs. McDonahue, but not as pretty, more repetitious. Instead of rising and falling in delightful and surprising ways, the notes just went up and up and up, higher and higher, then down and down and down, lower and lower.

Still, Toes was intrigued enough to creep up the stairs.

On the top step he peeked under the door but saw only the doorway and the bottom part of the darkened TV screen in a farther room. But up here the notes, monotonous as they were, penetrated him in a way the beautiful melodies in the McDonahues' living room never had, slicing right through his fur and ricocheting around his rib cage.

Suddenly his heart started beating faster than when he'd gotten his first whiff of fresh mouse. Instead of dull progressions, the sounds were now arranging themselves into marvelous patterns. The notes soared and swooped and soared again, so gorgeous they were almost painful. And though there was something deeply lonely about the sounds, they magically wiped his loneliness away.

5

The concert might have lasted two hours, or it might have lasted four, Toes wasn't sure. In a way, it was as if he'd been asleep. In another way, he'd never felt so wide-awake.

After the music ended, there was a sound of running water, followed by a long silence. Then the pant cuffs once more crossed Toes's field of vision, and he soon smelled the fishy smell again. The cuffs made another brief appearance, and the TV popped on. It was the newsman. Toes preferred the concert, but the TV was also good company, and he remained at the top of the stairs peering out under the door till the screen went dark.

Then he crept downstairs and crouched in a corner.

His stomach was rumbling again, and before long a plumpish mouse ventured out from under the stairs. But just as Toes was about to spring, a less plump mouse popped out and cried:

"If you'll be so kind as to whistle a tune, I'll show you some moves by the light of the moon."

To Toes's astonishment, the plump mouse actually started whistling—though in a very squeaky way—and the less plump one started doing a jig in the trapezoid of moonlight by the drain. This made them both easy pickings. But hungry as he was, Toes couldn't quite bring himself to slaughter them when they were having such a merry time.

Eventually Toes pushed one of the old shoes from the box over to the baseboard and blocked off the mousehole; then he crept around the edge of the room.

"So you come here to dance?" he said, emerging from under the stairs.

The two mice froze. Then they made a mad dash for the hole.

Instead they found the shoe.

"Don't worry," Toes said. "If I wanted to eat you, I would have done it already."

The trembling mice turned and stared across the basement at the cat blocking their path to the other hole.

"So this is your dance floor?" Toes asked.

The plump mouse gulped. "This is the best way from hither to yon," he squeaked.

"Sometimes we come here and dance until dawn," said the other.

Toes couldn't help admiring them for rhyming even with their lives in peril. "Hither to yon?" he said.

"There's food over here, and food over there," said the plump one.

"And this is our cold-weather thoroughfare," said the other.

"I see," Toes said. "They have garbage cans in the basements of the housing projects, and this is how you get between them."

"Put very nicely," said one.

"Very precisely," said the other.

"Well, listen," Toes said. "I'm stuck here. But I promise to let you pass through whenever you want if you'll do something for me."

"Compel us!" said one.

"Impel us!" said the other.

"Or better yet," said the first, "just tell us."

"Bring me some food from time to time," Toes said. "Spread the word among your friends. That way I won't be tempted to . . . "

"Overpower us?"

"Devour us?"

"Ingest us?"

"Digest us?"

"Exactly," Toes said.

As he stepped toward them, the plump mouse bolted to the southeast corner of the basement, the less plump one to the southwest. Toes shoved the shoe away from the hole, then recrossed the basement and headed up the stairs. When he was halfway up, the mice dashed to the newly exposed hole and dove through.

Toes had a strong feeling he would never

see them again—but before long their quivering whiskers poked out.

"I'm going to find you some aged Vermont cheddar," declared one.

"I'll get you some Roquefort," said the other, "and that's even better."

Over the next few days Toes made it clear to the mice that he wasn't as cheese mad as they were. This made their toll paying all the less painful. Whatever lovely scraps of cheese they scrounged out of the housing projects' garbage, they kept for themselves; Toes received lesser delicacies like half-gnawed chicken legs and fish bones. But even if these offerings weren't as tasty as fresh mouse, they filled his stomach and kept him from having to feel like a cold-blooded murderer.

Toes's days fell into a ritual. Sleeping late, the pole of sunlight—at least on sunny days—the lovely, nutty smell, the lonely dimming, the repetitious sounds, the glorious concert, the running water, the fish smell, the TV viewing, the midnight snacks from the basement-traversing mice. All he could ever see of the tenant upstairs was the pant cuffs and old tennis shoes, but he concluded that the person must be quite old because he or she had such regular habits and because the music tended to be heartrendingly sad—though in a funny way it was the sadness that cheered Toes up. "You may be lonely," the music seemed to say, "but trust me, the world contains loneliness deeper than yours."

Every day the two small windows supplied less and less light. But as if to make up for the shortening days, the furnace sprang to life, turning the basement nice and toasty. On TV, people started talking a lot about the Holidays, but this had no effect on the tenant's regular habits. There never seemed to be more than one set of footsteps, so Toes concluded that the person overhead lived alone and rarely entertained. It seemed a pity that he or she didn't care to share the beautiful music with anyone; but then, Toes was happy to be the secret sharer.

Eventually there was talk on TV of things

called valentines, but the tenant's routine remained unchanged—till one afternoon the concert abruptly ended, the lovely notes giving way to coughs. The coughs of a man. And of a man who was somehow creating the beautiful music himself, not just listening to it on a machine as Mrs. McDonahue had. For whenever she'd coughed or spoken, the music had simply continued.

But she'd never coughed as violently as this. The fit grew worse and worse, till Toes feared the old man was about to keel over and die. But while his hacks and coughs interrupted the next few afternoon concerts, the concerts continued, and gradually the coughing subsided.

Gradually, too, the days grew longer, and the furnace didn't come on so often. One night as he was about to doze off by the hot-water heater, Toes heard the gleeful squeaks of two of his favorite mice.

"Well, I admit this moonlight's okay in a pinch," said the plump one who whistled.

"But the dance floor's a matter of inch by

inch," said the less-plump one who danced.

"Out there you don't feel like a prisoner."

"Out there you can feel the moon right on your fur!"

Toes just smiled at their mousy silliness. But with each passing night the food deliveries became skimpier, and when the mice stopped appearing altogether, it dawned on him that the warming weather allowed them to use an outdoor passage between the housing projects. Who could blame them for preferring the great outdoors to this dreary basement?

But it didn't give Toes a cheerful springtime. He grew so starved that he resorted to eating putty. It didn't agree with him. In fact, it made him deathly ill. For three whole days he just lay around in a stupor. He couldn't even appreciate the concerts. And by the time the poison finally worked its way through his system, he was so feeble he could barely stand up.

Peering around, he decided to enlarge one of the mouseholes to escape his dungeon. He mustered his strength and managed to climb to the tool table and nudge the chisel to the edge. But if he pushed it off, it would clang on the concrete floor and alert the tenant. Toes climbed back down, positioned the old shoe near one of the table legs, dragged himself back up to the tabletop, and pushed the chisel off so that it landed on the shoe with a dull thud.

The chisel was too heavy and unwieldy for him to pick up in his mouth in his weakened state, but he managed to shove it over to the mousehole. Sawing proved very awkward. He spent an exhausting night and morning at it and hardly enlarged the hole at all. It was futile.

He had only one option left: to alert the tenant upstairs to his existence. It meant risking the Pound, but even that had to be better than starving to death. Unfortunately, the sawing had sapped him of his little remaining strength. He was too weak even to produce much of a meow. As another afternoon concert began, he inched his way over to the staircase and hauled himself up onto the first stair. He had to rest several minutes before attempting the next one. By the time he was halfway up, the concert was over.

He lay there depleted, listening to the faint sound of the running water. Then, after half an hour of silence, he got a whiff of the tantalizing fishy smell. It revived him a bit, and he struggled upward. But as soon as heaved himself onto the top stair, he passed out, utterly spent.

When he came to, the fishy smell had dissipated. Lifting his head, he peered under the door and saw a black-and-white movie on the TV. A murder mystery, it looked like. He didn't have the strength to give the door a bang, but he reached up and scratched it. Nothing happened. He meowed. But the meow was so meager he could barely hear it himself. Soon the TV screen turned blurry, and his head grew so heavy it sank down onto his paws.

A loud creak. A flicked switch. Cracking his eyes open, Toes blinked at a glaring light bulb dangling from the basement ceiling.

"Where in the world did you come from?"

Toes slowly swiveled his head. His eyes traveled up and up and up, from the toes of a pair of tennis shoes to a pair of baggy khakis to an untucked T-shirt to a thin face framed with long, uncombed hair as black as his own fur. To his surprise, the towering tenant wasn't old after all. Older than John McDonahue, but a lot younger than Mr. McDonahue. He was unshaven, and there was a glint of sadness in the dark, deep-set, down-peering eyes—the same sadness as in the music.

"Pardon me," the man said, stepping over him.

The man clomped down the basement stairs. Too weak to move, Toes just swiveled his head back the other way and watched.

"Haven't been down here in months," said the man, standing in the middle of the basement floor. He picked up one of the shoes, examined it curiously, tossed it into the box, then picked up the chisel. "You weren't using this, were you, cat?" he said, setting it on the table.

Toes couldn't even meow.

"So that's how you got in," the man said, noticing the back window.

The man picked up a hammer and nails, dragged the stool over to the window, and climbed up. Once he'd resecured the piece of Masonite over the window frame, he got down and went over to the wardrobe.

"Whew, strong moth balls," he said, turning his face away as he opened the door.

He pulled out a clothes bag and mounted the stairs. At the top he stepped over Toes again. But he didn't close the door behind him, and it wasn't long before Toes smelled something lovely. A bowl had landed by his snout. He managed to pull himself into a sitting position. The bowl was full of milk.

It didn't take him long to lap it all up. The bowl then rose up. It came back full again.

It was amazing how quickly two bowls of milk brought him back to life.

"Don't be a stranger," came the man's voice. "I could use a bit of company."

Toes climbed into a little hallway. To his left was a living room, not nearly as spacious or fancy as the McDonahues'. Lists of names were scrolling down the TV screen there, signifying the end of the murder mystery. In the kitchen, to his right, the man was pulling a dark suit out of the clothes bag.

"Come on in," he said, draping the suit over the back of one of two chairs pulled up to a kitchen table.

Toes made a halting entrance. The kitchen wasn't as fancy or spacious as the McDonahues' either, and though the floor was linoleum like theirs, corners of the squares were curled up or broken. The man crouched down and fingered the brass tag attached to Toes's collar.

"Toes? Is that your name? August fifth of last year, eh? That would make you about eight months old. Shame there's no address or phone number. I bet somebody misses you."

The man sat in a chair and patted a thigh, inviting Toes to hop up. Toes felt strong enough, but he didn't. He didn't want the man to notice his extra toes.

"I'm not going to hurt you," the man said,

reaching down and scooping Toes up into his lap. "My God, you're a bag of bones."

Toes's heart whirred. It felt wonderful to have his fur stroked after going untouched for so long, but he dreaded the inevitable discovery. Sure enough, the man examined his paws.

"So that's how you got your name. Funny, I was figuring you might be bad luck—black cat and all. But who knows, maybe you're a good sign. Seven's a lucky number, right?"

Relieved, Toes relaxed a bit. He even began to purr as the man smoothed the fur on his belly. After a while the man set him on the floor and got a carton out of the freezer. He scooped something into two bowls, setting one on the table and the other on the floor.

"To celebrate," he said. "You're my first company since Janice dumped me a year ago."

The thing in the bowl was awfully cold, but Toes licked it for a while to be polite. When the man finished his, he laughed and said, "So you're not a coffee ice cream junkie, eh? Tomorrow we'll get you some cat food."

Toes, who liked the way the man talked to him, trailed him into the living room. On a desk across from the TV was a computer like John McDonahue's. Beyond that, an open door revealed a bedroom with an inviting-looking bed, the rumpled blanket forming all sorts of cozy caves and hollows. But what caught Toes's eye most was an object perched in a chair by one of the living room windows. It was made of old, gleaming wood and had an hourglass shape and a slender black neck with four wires on it.

The man plunked down on a couch covered in faded brown corduroy and patted the cushion beside him. Toes hopped up. From there he could see the entire TV: quite a luxury after months of only the bottom third. Using a gizmo like the McDonahues', the man found another murder mystery and, as he watched, stroked Toes's fur.

He laughed when Toes propped his chin on his knee. "You'd think you were following the plot," he said, chucking Toes behind the ears. "Personally, I think the girlfriend did it, don't you? Oh, sorry, this I can't take." The man lowered the volume of the welling background music. "I apologize—I'm a terrible snob about music."

When the offending music petered out, the man increased the volume again. He did this several times in the course of the movie. Toward the end it became obvious, as Toes had suspected all along, that the murderer was the jealous brother, not the girlfriend.

"Shows what I know," the man said, yawning as he flicked off the TV. "You're welcome to sleep here, Toes. Or you can come sleep with me, if you want."

The man rose from the couch and turned out the lights in the kitchen and living room and went into the bedroom. He'd left the door to the basement ajar, so Toes went down and used the toilet. He stopped halfway back up the stairs, seeing the silhouette of the man looming at the top.

"I *thought* I'd been hearing water in the pipes. You've been using that toilet, haven't you?"

Toes cocked his head to one side, eyeing the man uncertainly.

"I'm not complaining," the man said. "It's . . . it's amazing. I'd heard of cats being toilet trained, but I had no idea you could learn to flush."

Ever since he'd grown long enough, Toes had been flushing, like the people in commercials.

"Come on," the man said, smiling. "Let's hit the hay."

Toes wasn't totally back to normal, so it took him a while to mount the stairs. In the dim kitchen he resampled the ice cream, which was melted now and not so cold. By the time he reached the bedroom doorway, the man was climbing into bed in his pajamas.

"Come on up, if you want," the man said.

Toes crossed a braided rug and hopped onto the foot of the bed.

"Sleep well," the man said, switching off the lamp.

Toes, who saw well in the dark, watched the man roll onto his left side. The man murmured,

"Night," to a framed photograph on the bedside table. Then he rolled the other way and, hugging a spare pillow, fell asleep. Toes wormed his way into a blanket cave near the sleeping man's feet, a place far softer and warmer than the basement—or, for that matter, than the McDonahues' utility room. He licked a creamy smudge off his snout and, curling up in a tight ball, purred himself to sleep.

6

Snug in his blanket grotto, Toes slept as soundly as when he was just a week old. He slept and slept and slept, until important-sounding voices finally broke in on his dreams. He yawned twice and crawled out of his cave to find the bedroom flooded with daylight.

Toes stretched, dropped lazily onto the braided rug, and padded through to the kitchen, where the man was sitting at the table with a mug of coffee, listening to news on the radio.

"Morning, sleepyhead," the man said. "I was just about to go run some errands."

The man stood up, flicked off the radio, and pulled a jacket off a peg. Toes walked over to him and nuzzled his ankle.

"You want to come along?"

The man pulled some keys out of a drawer and, picking up the suit of dark clothes he'd brought from the basement, ducked through a door leading into the garage. First he opened the garage door, filling the garage with daylight. Then he opened the door of the car—a car that could just about have fit in the back of the McDonahues' SUV. Toes eagerly hopped in ahead of him. The seats were vinyl, not leather, and the car had the nice, nutty smell.

But as soon as they pulled out onto the avenue, Toes cowered back in the passenger seat. Since he wasn't in a carrying case, there was nothing to shield him from the terrifying novelties in the windows: gigantic trucks with tattooed arms sticking out of the cabs, tall buildings glittering in the sun, a traffic helicopter that sounded like a machine gun in a gangster movie. The man, however, didn't seem to mind these things. He hummed a tune as he drove. This had a calming effect on Toes, at least until he spotted a flock of birds perched on some telephone wires. Heart racing, he made an instinctive lunge at them—and smacked his head on the glass, causing the man to laugh. A little chagrined, Toes just watched the world go by until the sight of a woman walking a Great Dane sent him diving under the seat, again making the man laugh.

Down there under the seat springs Toes discovered the source of the nutty smell: half a sandwich. The bread was moldy, but the brownish paste spread on it was quite tasty. When he'd eaten his fill, he climbed back up on the seat.

"That's where I'm auditioning Tuesday," the man remarked.

Toes got up on his hind legs and peered out the window at a stately domed building with a long front staircase leading up to four white columns.

"Philharmonic Hall," the man said. "You'll have to keep all those toes of yours crossed for me."

The man reached out and stroked a white furry thing dangling from the keys in the ignition. Toes moved over that way and gave the thing a curious swat.

"My lucky rabbit's foot," the man said. "Though come to think of it, that must seem kind of barbaric to you. I mean, it could almost be a cat's foot."

After another block they parked in front of a mini mall. The man put the rabbit's foot keys in his pocket and cracked the windows.

"Hold down the fort," he said, grabbing the suit of clothes from the backseat.

With the car stationary, Toes felt bold enough to hop up onto the back of the front seat. From there he watched the man carry the suit into a store. The man emerged empty-handed, went into another store, came out with a bag, walked into another store, came out with two bags.

When they got back to the house, the man unpacked the bags on the kitchen counter. One contained a big jar of the brownish paste, a half-dozen cans with pictures of fish on the side, a loaf of sliced bread, a bottle of milk, and a carton decorated with a picture of a freshly sliced orange. The other bag contained a dozen cans the same size as the ones with the pictures of fish but with pictures of grinning cats instead. He opened one of these, releasing a lovely aroma, and spooned the contents into a bowl.

"Hope you like Chicken and Liver Delight," he said, setting the bowl on the floor. "There's others if you don't."

Chicken and Liver Delight was truly delightful. Toes finished off about half of it, then licked his whiskers and ventured back into the living room. The man was sipping coffee in front of the computer. Toes rubbed the side of his head against the man's leg, and the man picked him up and set him in his lap.

"Liner notes," he said when Toes peeked at the computer screen. "That's what I do for a living—write liner notes for classical CDs. They're the descriptions of the composer and the composition and the musicians, in case cats don't bother to read them." He laughed softly.

"To tell you the truth, most people don't bother to read them either."

Toes perched happily in the man's lap till the man got up to refill his coffee mug, at which point Toes realized he needed to use the toilet. When he returned from the basement, the man was back at the computer.

"You know, Toes, you can use mine, if you want," the man said with a smile. "Long as you flush."

A couple of hours later Toes followed the man into the kitchen and watched him open the big new jar of brown paste. Out came the nutty smell. Toes sniffed the air greedily, and the man let him lick some paste off his finger.

"So you like peanut butter, eh? I'm beginning to think we're soul mates."

While the man ate his peanut butter sandwich, Toes nibbled Chicken and Liver Delight.

"Are you thirsty?" the man asked. "What have you been drinking, anyway?"

After setting a bowl of water by Toes's food dish, the man ventured down into the basement. When he returned, he was scratching the back of his tousled head.

"First you had to empty out the eye screws, then you got the can to the sink, then you turned the faucet. How'd you do all that?"

Toes meowed.

"What's that, cat for 'Necessity is the mother of invention'? You know, Toes, I should introduce myself. Sebastian Crabbe."

After lunch Toes followed Sebastian into the bedroom, where they both took naps. Again Toes slept longer, waking up only when he heard the repetitious notes. He slithered out of his blanket cave and, out in the living room, found Sebastian seated in the chair by the window with the beautiful wooden object under his chin. Toes plunked down in front of him and watched him pull a bow over the strings.

"Do you like the violin?" Sebastian asked, pausing.

Though Toes had never heard the word "violin," he meowed enthusiastically. Sebastian looked amused.

"In that case, enough scales," he said.

While Sebastian fooled around with something on a black metal stand, Toes hopped up onto a nearby armchair and saw that it was a page covered with tiny symbols that looked like the birds on the telephone wires. Also propped on the stand was a photo of a man older than Sebastian but bearing a resemblance to him, in spite of the fact that he was clean-shaven and very formally dressed.

"A little Vivaldi?" Sebastian said, taking up the bow again.

Toes was pretty sure Mrs. McDonahue had liked Vivaldi, but the music that came out of Sebastian's violin was far more resonant than anything he'd heard with her. It made his heart vibrate.

When Sebastian finished, Toes hopped down off his armchair and nudged Sebastian's ankle.

"Did you really enjoy that, Toes?"

Toes meowed.

"Want to hear my audition pieces?" Sebastian asked.

Toes meowed again.

"This one's Bach," Sebastian said, arranging some new music on the stand. "It's the chaconne from one of his partitas. It may not sound so hard, but believe me, it's devilish."

Toes had never heard of a chaconne, or a partita, but whatever they were, the music sounded far more angelic than devilish. In fact, if there was such a thing as a heaven for cats, the Bach took Toes there on a visit.

"This next one's Paganini," Sebastian said, changing the music on the stand. "Paganini was about the greatest violinist who ever lived."

The Paganini wasn't as heavenly as the Bach, but it was so exciting that Toes did a little jig like the mouse in the moonlight.

"I hope Feldman reacts that way," Sebastian said, smiling.

When his bow was moving really fast, it threw off a fine white powder, so when he finished playing, he carefully wiped the violin clean.

"Now for me," he said.

He disappeared into the bedroom, and soon Toes heard the familiar sound of running water, followed by silence. Toes ventured curiously into the bedroom—and was met by a sight as appalling as the burning orange skulls. There, through the open bathroom doorway, he saw Sebastian's head, perched on a mound of bubbles.

"What's the matter, Toes?" the head said.

Toes choked out a meow.

"I'm just taking a bath," the head said. "We're not as good at cleaning ourselves as you cats are, you know. And the hot water relaxes your fingers after practicing." The head smiled. "Is it the bubbles?" A hand poked out and tossed some bubbles in the air. "I know it's silly, but it's my way of being with Janice. She loved bubble baths."

In a few minutes, to Toes's immense relief, all of Sebastian emerged from the bubbles. He dried off and donned his usual clothes; then he flicked on the TV news and went into the kitchen. While he opened one of the cans with the fish on it, Toes squatted down to clean his bowl of his Chicken and Liver Delight. Soon Sebastian sat down to eat, and Toes hopped into the other chair. Nearly full-size now, he was able to put his front paws up on the edge of the table.

"Dinner conversation?" Sebastian said. "Well, I'd tell you about myself, since we seem to be living together—except there's not very much to tell. I write liner notes and play the fiddle. For lunch I eat a peanut butter sandwich. For dinner, tuna fish salad." He sampled the tuna salad. "If I weren't such a wimp, I'd be playing with the Philharmonic. My grandfather was the original concertmaster there—that's leader of the first violins, the most important chair in the orchestra. My father used to play with the Philharmonic, too. And my cousin Thaddeus is the current concertmaster. All I ever wanted was to be in the violin section, but last year I flunked my audition—for the second time. That's when Janice dumped me. You really can't blame her for getting fed up. She made it in her first try—Janice plays the flute. We used to do duets.

You haven't lived till you've played a duet, Toes." A dreamy look drove the sadness out of Sebastian eyes. "It's like . . . it's like you've escaped gravity. Like you've grown wings. I suppose it's inconsiderate to go on about it, seeing as cats can't make music, but, gosh, if you knew how much I miss our duets . . ."

Sebastian took a swig of water. Toes cocked his head inquisitively to one side.

"How'd I flop? Well, to be honest, the audition's pretty grueling. The whole orchestra's sitting there in the audience, and you have to stand up and play two pieces with no music. And the conductor's right in the middle of the front row—the maestro, Daniel Feldman. I don't think he's too wild about me. I have a feeling Thaddeus may have told him I'm a lightweight or something. My problem is I can't seem to resist looking at Thad. He's eight years older than I am—the great musical prodigy of my generation of Crabbes. He gets this look on his face . . . it's hard to describe. It's this subtle, pitying look. Ever since I was a little kid with my first fiddle, he would get that look when I played—kind of a curl of his lip. I know, I know, I shouldn't look at him. Or else I should just move to another city and try a different orchestra. Janice suggested that. But I grew up here—and the Philharmonic's a Crabbe tradition."

Sebastian reached into the neck of his T-shirt and pulled out a thin chain with a gold medal dangling from it. He turned the medal to show Toes both sides. The tail side was an image of Philharmonic Hall, with its four columns; the head side showed a man with a laurel wreath in his hair and a small harplike instrument in his hands.

"Orpheus," Sebastian said. "He's a great musician from Greek mythology. The orchestra gave this to my grandfather when he retired. It's solid gold. He passed it on to my father, and my father passed it on to me. So, you see, the Philharmonic's in my blood. It's a point of honor. Besides, to be a professional musician, you have to rise above letting things bother you." Sebastian swallowed another bite of tuna fish and smiled. "But Thad's not going to get to me this time. I've practiced all year with his picture staring me in the face. I'm ready." He reached across and patted Toes's head. "And now I've got you for a good luck charm. Tuesday's going to be great. It's got to be—it's my last chance. With the Philharmonic it's three strikes and you're out."

Toes, who had watched enough baseball with Mr. McDonahue to know exactly what that meant, meowed sympathetically. Sebastian hooted.

"If I didn't know better, I'd almost believe you understand every word I say!"

7

That weekend Toes was treated to a musical feast. Sebastian practiced his heart out, running through his audition pieces so many times, he didn't sit down to his tuna salad till ten o'clock. But on Monday the violin didn't wake Toes from his after-lunch nap. When he did wake up, he found that he was alone in the house. He parked himself hopefully at the foot of the music stand. But it wasn't till hours later, after dark, that Sebastian finally returned, carrying his suit of black clothes in a clear-plastic sheath.

"Sorry I was gone so long, Toes," he said, flicking on lights. "I was just going to the dry cleaners—then I got it in my head to drive out to the country. I took a long walk by the river. It kind of cleared my head for tomorrow."

The next morning Toes got out of bed along with Sebastian, who took his bath hours early. Then Sebastian covered his cheeks with white lather and shaved off his scruffy whiskers. Once he combed his long hair neatly and donned the dark suit, Toes thought he looked very handsome.

"Janice used to help me with this," Sebastian said, struggling with a black bow tie in the dresser mirror. "I was kind of hoping she'd call last night to wish me luck, but she didn't."

Toes went up and nudged Sebastian's ankle.

"Thanks, Toes. I'll bet you could tie one of these things if you had to."

Sebastian fed Toes but had no breakfast himself, just a mug of coffee, which he carried out to the living room and set on the windowsill. He tuned his violin, took a gulp of coffee, played a few scales, took a gulp of coffee, played a few arpeggios, took a gulp of coffee, then loosened the hairs on his bow and stuck it and the violin and the removable chin rest into a black case lined with rich green velvet. He looked over the music on the stand, stared at the photo of his cousin, went into the bedroom and straightened his tie, then carried his violin case into the kitchen.

"Don't forget," he said, opening the door to the garage. "All twenty-eight toes."

When Sebastian was gone, Toes tried to cross his toes for luck, but he couldn't. Too nervous to eat much, he went and sat in Sebastian's playing chair and stared at the photo of Sebastian's cousin. After a while, he put his front paws up on the windowsill and peered out at the weedy little backyard. The aisle of sky between the ten-story housing projects was blue, which seemed a good sign. And as he watched, a cloud sailed by that was shaped very much like a violin, which seemed even better.

Still, Toes wished with all his heart that he was in Philharmonic Hall. It wasn't so far away: he remembered from the car trip. Suddenly he remembered something else. A conversation he'd overheard between two mice one wintry night when hailstones were pelting the basement windows.

"Ouch, what a blow!"

"My whole body's in pain."

"It's harder than snow."

"It's harder than rain."

"Lucky that shingle's loose under the sink—though a pity the trash has to make such a stink."

Toes hopped down off the chair and scampered into the kitchen. Standing on his hind legs, he managed to open the little door to the shadowy cabinet underneath the sink. He stepped inside and skirted the tuna-smelling trash can. It was dark behind it, but he located a hole in the wall. It was fine for mice but a little too small for a cat to squeeze through.

A couple of times that weekend Toes had taken up Sebastian's invitation to use the upstairs toilet, but Sebastian still left the basement door ajar for him. Toes pattered down to the basement now. There was no longer any need to worry about noise, so he climbed to the tool table and nudged the chisel off the edge. It clanged on the stone floor.

Heavy as it was, he found the balancing point in the center and started up the stairs with it in his mouth. The weight made his jaws ache. He had to set the chisel down six times on the way up.

In all it took nearly an hour to get back behind the trash can with the tool. Again the sawing was slow work, but little by little he enlarged the hole a bit. He poked his head in. He could tell by where the edges of the hole hit his whiskers that his body still wouldn't fit through. He chiseled more, did the whisker test, chiseled more, did another whisker test. Another hour passed before he could squeeze through into the wall itself. A needle of sunlight led him over to the loose shingle. He butted it with his nose, and it swung up like a mini version of the garage door.

There was the backyard: the dented aluminum garbage can, the rusty table and chair, a chain-link fence beyond covered with a straggly creeper. Toes popped out and headed down the litter-choked passageway between the house and the building next door. But just as he came out onto the little front yard, Sebastian's car swung into the driveway.

Toes raced back around to the rear of the house and emerged from the cabinet under the sink just as Sebastian stomped into the kitchen. Toes's heart sank. Sebastian's bow tie was undone, his face grim. He dumped his violin case and car keys and a brown paper bag on the table and slumped in a chair.

Sebastian didn't say hello or anything else till Toes hopped up onto the other chair and put his paws on the table edge. Then he muttered:

"You should have been there. You would have had a good laugh."

Sebastian pulled a tall bottle of amber liquid from the bag, unscrewed the top, and took a swig right from the bottle. He winced at the taste, but it didn't keep him from lifting the bottle and taking another swig.

"Well, that's over and done with, anyway," he said, plunking the bottle down. "Pity you weren't there for the Bach. I was a star. Easy as pie. But then . . ."

He picked up the bottle, tilted his head back, and took several gulps, his Adam's apple bobbing up and down. When he set the bottle back down, it was nearly half empty.

All of a sudden he scraped his chair back and marched out of the room. Toes hopped down to follow, but in no time Sebastian was back with the framed photo from his bedside table. He flung open the back door and lunged outside. Toes reached the doorway just in time to see him hurl the framed photo into the garbage can, to the accompaniment of shattering glass.

When Sebastian sat back down at the table, he was grinning in a way that was new to Toes. It reminded him of the horrible leering grins on the orange heads he'd seen in windows the night he'd come here.

"Good riddance," Sebastian said, and then he took another long swig from the bottle.

Toes knew it wasn't polite to get up on tables except at the vet's, but he did so anyway. He skirted the violin case and started licking Sebastian's right hand. Sebastian hooted.

"That's the one, Toes." He held up his other hand. "This one was fine and dandy. The old fingering was perfecto, if I do say so myself. It's the bowing did me in." His voice was getting as strange as his grin. "Middle of the Paganini—boing! There goes the old E string. Should have put on a new one this morning—but it happens. Not the end of the world. Strings break. Feldman goes, 'Not to worry, Mr. Crabbe. Just replace it and start over from the beginning of the last theme.' So Mr. Crabbe puts on a new string. Takes a minute. That's when Mr. Crabbe makes his big birdbrain boo-boo. Till then Mr. Crabbe hasn't looked at any of the musicians. Not once. They're all sitting out there, but he's focused on the music. Then he starts thinking of this time he was playing with Janice—Stravinsky—and boing goes the old E string. So he checks for her in the audience. She's right next to Thad. Right next to him! Or he's next to her. And just at that second the creep's leaning over and whispering something in her ear, and she has to cover her mouth to keep from laughing. Bingo. The old right hand clenched up in a fist. No feel after that. None. Pathetic."

By now Toes was extremely suspicious of the amber liquid, but he could lick only one hand at a time, so Sebastian had the other to pick up the bottle with. After taking another slug, he smacked the bottle back down on the table so hard, it made Toes jump.

"I'll show him," Sebastian muttered.

The chair scraped back, and out of the room he marched. Toes got to the living room just in time to see Sebastian grab the photo off the music stand and rip it to shreds.

As the last piece drifted to the floor, Sebastian turned and staggered toward Toes. Back in the kitchen Sebastian stood swaying slightly, eyes fixed on his violin case.

"That's the ticket," he said, the strange grin returning to his face. "His precious Strad."

Toes hopped up on the table and meowed.

"What's his Strad? His fiddle. Made by a man called Stradivarius, three hundred years ago. Used to be our grandfather's, but now it's Thad's. Ha, ha, Thad's Strad."

Sebastian beamed as if this was a brilliant rhyme, but frankly Toes thought it was even sillier than the mice's.

"He lives in the burbs," Sebastian said. "I'll drive out and smash it to bits."

So saying, Sebastian took another drink, then flung open the basement door and clattered down the stairs. When he lurched back into the kitchen, he had a hammer in his hand. He went through the door into the garage, and Toes heard the car door open. But it didn't close.

"Keys," Sebastian said, stepping back into the kitchen.

The keys lay by his violin case. Toes grabbed the rabbit's foot between his teeth, leaped off the table, tore into the living room, and dove under the couch.

He was huddled against the baseboard, the

rabbit's foot clamped in his jaws, when one side of the couch swung out from the wall, exposing him. He dashed out from under the other end of the couch and ducked into the bedroom.

"Give me those keys!" Sebastian roared, stomping after him.

As Toes dove under the bed, Sebastian slammed the bedroom door, cutting off any possible escape route. But Toes didn't really need one. It was a large bed, and every time Sebastian went around to one side and groped underneath, Toes simply scooted over to the other. As this game went on, Sebastian grew clumsier and clumsier, his angry mutterings thicker and thicker. Finally the box spring let out a great creak. No more Sebastian.

Toes remained where he was, the rabbit's foot clamped in his mouth. But there was so much dust under the bed—Sebastian was not much of a housekeeper—that Toes started sneezing. It got so bad that he finally had to drop the keys and creep out onto the braided rug. Up above, Sebastian's feet dangled over the edge of the bed, one shoe on, one shoe off. Toes let out a tentative meow. Sebastian didn't so much as twitch. Toes hopped up onto the foot of the bed. Sebastian was lying there passed out in his tuxedo, which was now smeared with dust.

Sebastian's breathing was very raspy, and for a while Toes kept an anxious watch over him. But after all his worrying and chiseling and hide and seek, he was pretty exhausted himself, so eventually he burrowed into a blanket cave and fell asleep.

He was chasing a rabbit around the McDonahues' backyard when a hand closed around his middle. For a moment, he thought it was going to crush him; then the hand started gently stroking his fur. Sebastian's hand.

After a while, the hand withdrew and Sebastian murmured: "Sleep as long as you want, Toes."

Toes crawled out of his cave. The bedroom was bright with morning light; Sebastian was standing by the foot of the bed in his usual khakis and T-shirt. His eyes were a little bloodshot, but he was smiling his mild smile, not the maniacal one.

"I owe you a huge apology, Toes. And my heartfelt thanks. I don't remember everything about last night, but I think I've put most of it back together. I wanted to go smash Thad's violin, right? That's why there's a hammer on the roof of the car?"

Toes meowed.

"But you hid the car keys. Where are they?"

Toes dropped down onto the floor and entered the dim, dusty domain under the bed. When he came out with the rabbit's foot in his mouth, Sebastian whistled.

"Unbelievable." Sebastian sank down on the edge of the bed and took the keys. "I'm beginning to think you're some sort of freak of nature."

Toes winced.

"I don't mean freak in a bad way." Sebastian scooped Toes up into his lap. "I just mean you're incredibly smart." He rubbed Toes's belly. "A lot smarter than I am, evidently. How'd you get to be so intelligent?"

Toes purred.

"All I know is if you hadn't hidden these keys, I'd either be in jail or in the hospital. The car would probably be wrapped around a streetlamp somewhere. Or worse, I might have hit someone. The more I think about it . . ."

He leaned down and gave Toes a kiss between the ears.

"Hey, are you hungry?"

Sebastian got up and carried him into the kitchen. He opened a can of cat food and spooned some into his bowl.

"Salmon Supreme," he said, setting the bowl on the floor. "Hope you like it."

Salmon Supreme was even better than Chicken and Liver Delight.

"Maybe I ought to eat something, too," Sebastian said. "Maybe it'll help with this headache." He picked up the nearly empty bottle of amber liquid from the table. "I give you permission to shoot me if I ever touch that stuff again," he said, tossing it into the trash can under the sink.

He got his peanut butter out of the cupboard, fixed a sandwich, and poured himself a glass of milk. Once Toes had had his fill of salmon, he cleaned his whiskers, hopped up onto a chair, and put his paws on the edge of the table.

"Had enough?" Sebastian asked.

Toes meowed.

"Anything else I can do for you?"

Again Toes put aside good manners and climbed onto the tabletop. He nudged the violin case.

"Oh, please, anything but that," Sebastian said.

Toes nudged the case again.

"You know what Feldman said after I botched the Paganini? He said, 'Thank you for giving us a chance to hear you again, Mr. Crabbe. You do have a wonderful sound. But in an orchestra the crucial thing is dependability. Best of luck in your future endeavors.' At that moment I knew I'd never pick up a fiddle again. I knew it in my soul."

Toes gave the violin case such a push that it hit Sebastian's plate. Sebastian sighed.

"Well, I guess I can't refuse you, after what you did for me."

Toes hopped off the table. In the little hallway by the basement door he looked over his shoulder. Sebastian got out of his chair and picked up the violin case. Toes led the way into the living room and perched among the bits of torn photo at the foot of the music stand. Sebastian came over and sat down in his playing chair and drew his violin and bow out of the case.

As soon as he pulled the bow across the second highest string, the A string, it sounded as if he had an echo. He lowered his bow and gaped out the window.

"Minerva!"

As Sebastian opened the sash, Toes hopped up onto the nearby armchair and saw a bird with soft-brown feathers and an elegant neck perched on the ledge just outside the window. Instinctively he crouched to pounce.

"Now, Toes, I know cats like to go after birds," Sebastian said. "But Minerva's an old friend of mine. She comes back every spring. Her coo's a perfect A. She's better than a tuning fork."

For the moment, at least, Toes conquered his impulse to leap at the bird, but he couldn't help letting out a strangled meow that caused the dove to lift her pretty head in alarm and look left and right.

"Don't worry, Minerva, Toes won't hurt you." Sebastian picked up his bow and violin again. "I guess this is a sign. From now on, I'll have to settle for an audience of two. What would you guys like? A little Mozart?"

Among the new words Toes had picked up from Sebastian over the past week was a strange one: *brio*. "I sure didn't play that with much *brio*," Sebastian had muttered on more than one occasion. What "*brio*" meant, Toes had deduced, was "feeling." And now, as Sebastian launched into the Mozart, there was no *brio* at all. He hit every note and played and in perfect time—all the eighth notes half as long as the quarter notes—but the result was as limp and soggy as cat food left out too long in the bowl.

During the third movement, however, something happened. It was as if Sebastian couldn't hold out any longer against the music. Instead of sitting bolt upright with his violin at a stiff ninety-degree angle from his chest, he tilted the instrument down and swooped it back up, swaying rhythmically backward and forward. His playing grew livelier and livelier, more and more modulated, zipping from *pianissimo*—soft and quiet—to *fortissimo*—strong and loud. By the final movement, he was playing with all his usual zest, and Toes could feel the music to the tips of his twenty-eight toenails.

After finishing with a flourish, Sebastian lowered the violin slowly to his lap and blinked around him as if he wasn't sure where he was. Minerva cooed. Sebastian's eyes shifted out the window. Toes walked up and nudged Sebastian's ankle.

Instead of reaching down and stroking Toes's fur, Sebastian laid his bow across the music stand and pulled out the fine chain from inside his T-shirt. He undid the clasp and slipped off the gold medal. Reaching down, he removed Toes's collar. It took Sebastian a minute, but he managed to add the gold piece to the ring that held Toes's brass name tag. Then he bent down and refastened the collar around Toes's neck.

9

After his playing session Sebastian took his usual bath, but without bubbles.

The next day it poured as hard as the day Toes had tumbled into the basement, and Sebastian moped around with the TV blaring, never touching his violin. But on Thursday the sun came back out, and at around three in the afternoon, Minerva started cooing on the windowsill. Toes immediately assumed his post at the foot of the music stand. Soon Sebastian sat down and pulled his violin and bow out of the case and played the A string.

"Flat," he murmured. "All that rain."

He opened the window, making Minerva's

A clearer. This also gave Toes a clearer view of the bird, and somehow the gentleness in her eyes defused his desire to pounce on her.

"How long have you known Sebastian?" Toes asked.

To his surprise, the dove completely ignored him. She just cooed and cocked her head to watch Sebastian twist pegs on his violin.

"How about a little of Verdi's Requiem?" Sebastian said dryly. "A requiem for my career. And my dreams of getting Janice back."

It was a mournful concert, but Toes loved it anyway. The dove seemed to enjoy it, too, and even though she'd ignored his question, Toes couldn't help feeling something of a bond with her. Afterward, when Sebastian went off to take his nonbubble bath, Toes made another attempt at conversation.

"Have you ever heard anyone play so beautifully?" he asked.

But again Minerva refused to answer, simply letting out one of her coos.

Over the next few weeks, it became clear

that the two of them had different tastes in music. Minerva cooed most contentedly when Sebastian played romantic music, especially Tchaikovsky, whereas Toes preferred Bach. But Toes suspected the dove's refusal to talk to him was based less on this than simple jealousy. After all, he got to live in the house with Sebastian. And at the end of almost every concert, Sebastian played a little Bach air in his honor.

On the fifth of August, Sebastian played an all-Bach program and afterward presented Toes with a fish-flavored birthday treat. As he gobbled it down, a hazy image took shape in his mind: a curious contraption containing the same sort of delicacy. His early memories had dimmed, and since moving up out of the basement, he'd hardly given his former owners a thought. But there was one very early memory that would never fade away.

"Minerva," he blurted out, turning to the open window, "have you ever flown over a backyard with a white stake between two bushes?"

But once again Minerva refused to answer, mocking his question with one of her cloying coos. After that, he decided to give up on the uppity dove once and for all, tolerating her presence only because Sebastian seemed fond of her.

On a crisp October afternoon a couple of months later, Minerva failed to appear on the windowsill.

"Guess she had to fly south," Sebastian said with a sigh.

Toes felt like doing another mousy jig, but he contented himself with a gratified meow. So things returned to normal, Sebastian playing for him alone, and as the chilly months went by, Toes totally forgot about the dove. Then one afternoon that next April, a coo led Sebastian to throw up the sash.

"Minerva! You're back!"

It had been so long that Toes had also forgotten his resolution. "Minerva," he blurted out, "where have you been all this time?"

But the dove, it seemed, hadn't buried her grudge. She responded with no more than one of her infuriating coos.

"You're lucky I don't have you for dinner," Toes muttered under his breath.

And so it went. From April till October, Sebastian played for Toes and the haughty dove. From October till April, Toes had Sebastian to himself. As the seasons went by, it seemed to Toes that Sebastian's music swelled with ever sadder beauty, ever more beautiful sadness, and he longed for Sebastian to audition again, even if it meant trying out for an orchestra other than the Philharmonic. But in spite of his meaningful nudges, Sebastian took his violin out of the little house only once: to have the bridge replaced by somebody named Kreisler at the music store.

With the passing seasons Sebastian didn't change much. Sometimes he would let his whiskers grow, but never too long, for it's hard to tuck a violin under your chin with a beard. He rarely shopped for clothes, so his khakis and T-shirts and sweaters got dingier and more tattered, but his messy hair remained dark and thick. Minerva didn't change much, either, remaining aloof as ever—though one incident made Toes wonder if perhaps the dove disliked him less than he'd imagined. It was a hot summer day, and before sitting down to his computer, Sebastian opened several windows and the back door. Toes wandered out into the backyard and sprawled on the concrete. Soon he dozed off in the blissful warmth. He was having a wonderful dream of falling into a vat of fish treats—only to be awakened by a ruckus. It was Minerva. She was perched atop the chain-link fence, cooing her head off. Toes was about to tell her off when he saw, not two feet away, a striped snake coiled up, its green eyes fixed on him, its forked tongue darting in and out of its mouth. It was hard to know if the snake was poisonous or not, but Toes didn't wait around to find out, dashing back into the kitchen. Later on, when they all settled in for that day's concert, Toes thanked the dove for looking out for him. Of course, she didn't say, "You're welcome," but even so Toes felt more tolerant of her from that day on.

As for him, he didn't change much either—till he hit about four. Then he began putting on a little weight. His stomach started sagging a bit, and it wasn't quite so easy to hop up onto chairs. So in the mornings, while Sebastian was writing his liner notes, Toes would spend about twenty minutes running up and down the basement stairs. This helped, though Sebastian, who could hear the name tag and the gold medal clinking on Toes's collar, teased him about his "exercise fad."

Unlike Sebastian's whiskers, Toes's whiskers never grew, so he never had to worry about shaving. But one wintry morning when he was six, Sebastian noticed that their tips were graying.

"What's going on, Toes? You're way too young to be going gray."

One evening a few weeks later, Toes was watching the local news on TV while Sebastian was fixing his tuna salad in the kitchen. The newscaster began interviewing a friendly-looking woman with a silver streak in her hair whom he identified as Maria DeSilvero, the newly appointed conductor of the Philharmonic.

"Of course I'll never be able to fill Maestro Feldman's shoes," the woman said, "but I'm going to do my best."

"I understand you have a trademark baton, Ms. DeSilvero," said the newscaster.

"It probably sounds like the height of vanity, but my father made it specially for me when I first started out. He was a silversmith. It's silver plated. A little heavier than an ordinary baton, but I've gotten used to it."

By now Toes was meowing like crazy.

"Yeah, I heard," Sebastian said, coming into the living room. "But it doesn't affect me. They gave me my three shots." He sat down and started rubbing Toes's belly with a tuna-smelling hand. "Besides, all that's ancient history. I've resigned myself to never getting ahead. I'm not a true Crabbe, just a fiddler crab. It's sideways for me." He chucked Toes behind the ears. "Anyway, I don't need a big audience. I've got you."

Toes couldn't help purring at this.

One morning in June, Toes felt a twinge in his left hind leg during his stair climb. He didn't let it cut his workout short, but when he curled up on the foot of Sebastian's bed that night the twinge blossomed into a throb. It kept him awake for several hours, and the next morning he was so sleep deprived, he skipped his exercise entirely. That night the ache was milder, so he slept better and returned to the basement the next morning. But on his second ascent, the twinge came back, sharper than before.

He started skipping morning exercise, and as the summery days went by, his appetite diminished. He enjoyed the smell of his food but didn't really feel like gobbling it down, so all he did was lick it. Sebastian soon noticed.

"Don't you like Chicken and Liver Delight anymore, Toes? Want to try some of this new kind, with beef and cheese?"

To keep Sebastian from worrying, Toes filled his mouth with beef and cheese, but later he went down to the basement and deposited it by one of the mouseholes. As he grew skinnier, he took to fluffing up his fur with his tongue, also to keep Sebastian from worrying. But one morning in July, Sebastian scooped him up to put him in his lap under the computer table.

"Toes!" he cried. "You're a skeleton!"

Sebastian immediately went online and found a veterinarian. Half an hour later they were in an examination room. It wasn't the one where Toes had been tortured as a kitten, and the vet was a woman with blond hair, not a hairy-handed man. But the smells were similar.

Except for jabbing him with a needle, the

vet was quite gentle. “He didn’t get shortchanged in the toe department, I see,” she said, checking his paws. “I don’t feel any nodes or cysts on the old guy.”

“He’s not old,” Sebastian said.

“What is he, around fourteen?”

“He’s not even seven! He’ll be seven in, let’s see, nine days, on August fifth. That’s not old for a cat, is it?”

“Not generally. But some cats are shorter lived than others.”

She promised to call with the results of Toes’s blood tests and recommended a brand of cat food for older cats with digestive problems. Sebastian swung by the pet store on the way home to pick some up. Toes made a point of filling his mouth with the new food, but when Sebastian wasn’t looking, he again snuck down to the basement and deposited it by the mousehole. As he was dragging himself back up the stairs, he heard squeaky voices at his back.

“Thanks for remembering us.”

“And for not dismembering us.”

The next day the vet called Sebastian to report that the blood tests revealed no particular problem besides slight anemia. Sebastian went straight out to the grocery store and bought their finest cut of steak, a luxury he never would have allowed himself. He cooked the filet mignon under the broiler, cut it up into tiny pieces, and served it to Toes on his best china. It was so irresistibly delicious that Toes actually ate a bit. But he stuffed the rest in his mouth and took it down for the mice.

Though they were having a heat wave, that night Toes couldn't get warm even in his blanket cave. Instead of sleeping, he shivered—and worried about what would happen if he died. He realized he was genuinely glad of Minerva's existence. Till fall she would be around to listen to Sebastian's music. But what about when she flew south for the winter? With no audience, would Sebastian give up his playing? Somehow Toes found this thought heartbreaking.

Next afternoon, while Sebastian was tuning

his violin to Minerva's coo, Toes curled up in the armchair instead of perching at the foot of the music stand. It was warmer up there, but even so he succumbed to an attack of the shivers.

"For goodness' sake, Toes," Sebastian said, setting down his violin. "It's eighty-five degrees out."

From the back of the sofa, Sebastian got the afghan his mother had crocheted for him and tucked it around the skinny cat.

"Warmer?"

Toes meowed gratefully as he burrowed under the afghan. Sebastian returned to his tuning. After doing his scales, he said, "I don't know about you guys, but I'm in the mood for a little Scarlatti."

Being hidden from view gave Toes an idea. Once Sebastian was fully absorbed in the Scarlatti, Toes wriggled out from under the afghan, slipped off the chair, and snuck into the kitchen. He opened the door under the kitchen sink and ducked in behind the garbage can. The hole he'd enlarged with the chisel years ago was still there, and in his new emaciated condition he slipped through with ease. He pushed up the shingle and dropped out into the backyard.

The direct sunlight, though painfully bright, felt wonderful. He crouched there, letting it worm into his fur, and before long it had chased the ache out of his hindquarters. Off he went, pattering down the passageway between the house and the housing project. Out on the sidewalk he turned left, toward the city center.

If TV had taught him anything, it was that human beings infinitely prefer driving to walking, but every now and then one of them happened along on foot, forcing him to scoot behind a bush or dive under a parked car. At intersections, he waited patiently for the light—though, even so, a bike messenger nearly ran him down on one crosswalk. And a couple of blocks farther on, a Chihuahua yapped at him ferociously from the window of a town house. But at least he didn't encounter any skeletons or goblins.

After six or seven blocks he began to feel overheated and had to hunch in the shade of a trash can, his breathing coming too quickly. Eventually he cooled down enough to continue on.

Philharmonic Hall proved to be more of a journey than it had seemed by car, but he finally reached the foot of the grand front steps. As he ascended them, he felt twinges in *both* hind legs, and once he reached the sunlit portico, he found the big red front doors closed. He kept a watch over them from behind the base of one of the columns. After a while a door swung open, and out strode a bald man wheeling a violin case like Sebastian's except ten times bigger. Toes made a dash for it, but the door swung shut before he could slip inside.

He stationed himself nearer the doors, behind a tall cylinder around which cigarette ashes and grains of sand were scattered. The sand made for excellent traction, and the next time one of the doors opened, Toes shot through. Unfortunately, he didn't think to lift his eyes. So he didn't see that the human being who had walked out was the very one he was looking for: the new conductor, with the silver streak in her hair.

Toes found himself in a lobby with a shiny marble floor and a haunting musical echo. Not of a violin: the sound was more hollow and metallic. It was hard to determine the source, but the marble chilled his paws, so he didn't dawdle. As he crossed the lobby, the music grew louder. He scooted through an arched doorway—and stopped in his tracks.

Never in his life had he been in such an awe-inspiring space. Jutting out over rows of seats upholstered in rich gold velour were ornately gilded balconies gleaming under glittering chandeliers suspended from a ceiling where winged cupids peeked out from behind billowing pinkish-yellow clouds. At the far end of this heavenly place was a stage fit for a choir of angels—though just now there was only a plump-cheeked man playing a large brass horn and a skinny woman listening with a snakelike black instrument in her lap.

The carpeted aisle was much warmer than the lobby, but when the two musicians put away their instruments and walked off into the wings of the stage, Toes turned and padded back out onto the chilly marble, afraid he might get locked up in Philharmonic Hall overnight. Soon footsteps reverberated in the lobby: the two musicians, carrying their instrument cases. When they walked out of one of the front doors, Toes scuttled after them onto the portico.

Discouraged and sapped, he had to rest once a block on the trip home. There weren't many more people on the sidewalks than earlier, but it was a Monday, and the rush-hour traffic made the intersections perilous. Halfway home, a truly horrific sight loomed up ahead of him: a man walking not one but *two* Russian wolfhounds. The enormous beasts spotted him and started barking and straining against their leashes. A terrified Toes made a dash for the median strip of the avenue and narrowly missed being squashed by a brown UPS van. He crouched under a park bench, trembling from his snout to the tip of his tail till the dogs were well out of sight.

When Toes finally reached the backyard of the little house, he barely had the strength to lift the loose shingle and climb in behind the trash can. He had to rest a couple of minutes before making his way out from under the sink and creeping into the living room. Sebastian had come to the climax of a piece, his bow and fingers a blur. Toes didn't have the strength to hop into the armchair, and if he'd had only ten front claws, he probably wouldn't have been able to pull himself up. But fourteen just did the job. He slithered under the afghan and passed out.

A few minutes later Sebastian set down his violin.

"What did you think, old man?" he said, dabbing his brow with his handkerchief.

The usual enthusiastic meow wasn't forthcoming, so Sebastian walked over to the easy chair and lifted the afghan.

"That boring, eh?"

Chagrined, Sebastian looked over at the window. Minerva was cooing away on the outer ledge.

"Well, at least I didn't put *you* to sleep," he said.

11

When Toes slept through his dinner, Sebastian's chagrin turned to concern. Toes slept right through their usual TV-watching session, too. Carrying him into the bedroom, Sebastian was appalled at how light the cat felt. He made him a nice cozy womb in the blanket at the foot of the bed, and first thing in the morning he called the vet.

"I'm afraid there's not much we can do," she said. "It sounds to me as if Toes is winding down."

"Winding down?"

"Getting ready to die."

"But he's not even seven!"

"As I said, some cats live longer than others. Has he overexerted himself lately? Done anything unusual?"

"No, he's just been lazing around the house. He's even been skipping his morning exercise."

"Morning exercise?"

"He runs up and down the basement stairs in the morning to keep fit."

The vet laughed. "He's just chasing something. Cats don't exercise."

Sebastian decided not to pursue the subject. "He's lost all kinds of weight."

"Does he eat the new food?"

"Some. But he seems to prefer steak."

"Well, who wouldn't?"

As soon as he got off the phone, Sebastian went out to the grocery store and bought a couple more filets mignons. He put one in the broiler as soon as he got home, and the smell of it cooking finally roused Toes. He still felt bone weary from his trek to the concert hall, but he dropped down off the bed and padded into the kitchen.

"You're up!" Sebastian said, delighted. "You're okay, aren't you, Toes? You wouldn't go and leave me all alone, would you?"

Once again Sebastian cut the steak into morsels and served them on good china. Toes ate what little he could very deliberately, and when Sebastian left the kitchen, he filled his mouth and opened the little door under the sink and spat the steak out into the backyard. He certainly didn't feel up to attempting the journey back to Philharmonic Hall that day. And the next day was rainy, as was the next. But the sun returned on Friday, and for breakfast Toes nibbled a bit of steak and drank most of his bowl of water.

At concert time, he climbed onto the armchair but didn't burrow under the afghan. Sebastian opened the window and proceeded to tune his violin to Minerva's A.

"A little Chopin today, Toes?" he asked after doing his scales.

Toes was silent.

"No?" Sebastian said. "Some Corelli?"

Toes remained silent.

"Okay, okay, Bach it is."

No reaction.

"Not Bach? What do you want then? Another of the B's?"

Toes meowed.

"Brahms?"

Silence.

"Beethoven?"

Toes meowed enthusiastically.

"You want me to have to work, eh?" Sebastian said, smiling. "Okay, Beethoven it is."

As Sebastian dug out some music and started to play, Toes burrowed under the afghan. But as soon as he could tell that Sebastian was caught up in his playing, he slithered out and slipped into the kitchen.

The recent rain had turned the passageway between the house and the building dank, but otherwise today's journey to Philharmonic Hall went more smoothly than Monday's. Knowing exactly how far it was, Toes paced himself—and the only dog he encountered the whole way was a white-snouted dachshund who was so old, she could barely see or smell. Moreover, when Toes completed the exhausting hike up Philharmonic Hall's front steps, he found one of the doors propped open. This may have been to let in fresh air, but it also let out a gush of music so powerful, it nearly knocked the skeletal cat backward.

Toes forged on across the lobby, into the heavenly concert hall. The entire orchestra was practicing away on the stage. The largest section had violins like Sebastian's, led by a man resembling the one in the photo once propped on Sebastian's music stand. A smaller group played slightly larger violins. Others were playing violins so large, they had to hold them between their legs instead of under their chins, and in the very rear two men and a woman had to stand on their feet to play violins as big as they were. There were woodwinds of every variety, and all sorts of brass horns, including one that grew and shrank. Two men were banging drums; another played a dainty little triangle between a golden-haired woman strumming a harp and a bug-eyed man holding two brass cymbals high in the air. All the musicians had stands like Sebastian's, but when they weren't reading their music, their eyes all turned to a woman perched on a stool, front and center, with her back to Toes.

The more dramatically the conductor waved her silver stick, the more thunderous the music grew—till the cymbal player finally smashed the cymbals together three times in a row. Then the conductor set her baton on her music stand, and the musicians stopped playing. For a moment the gorgeous hall still rang. Then, silence.

"Thank you, everyone," the conductor said, getting off her stool. "The strings were a little limp in the staccato section, but otherwise pretty good. Let's take ten minutes and give it another run-through."

She strode off into the wings, and most of the members of the orchestra followed her example, setting their instruments aside and walking offstage. A few remained behind, paging back through their music or tinkering with strings or reeds; but they didn't stop Toes, who knew he would never have the strength for another trip to this glorious place. He hurried down the long aisle and, getting a running start, hopped up onto the stage. Or tried to. A few weeks ago he would have made it with ease. Today he didn't even come close.

Disgusted by his feebleness, he eyed one of the golden front-row seats. Could he use that as a jumping-off spot to reach the stage? But looking farther down the row of seats, he saw a better solution: a set of steps leading right up to the side of the stage.

Toes mounted these and followed the footlights to the slightly raised conductor's platform. A few weeks ago he would have had no problem jumping up onto the seat of the stool, but now he had to climb it like a ladder, digging his fourteen front claws into the first wooden cross brace to hoist himself up, then repeating the process. Scaling the stool so exhausted him that he sprawled gasping on the seat before moving on to the next step. This was the music stand—and here fortune favored him. It was well within reach. He rested his front paws on the little shelf and, sticking out his scratchy tongue, touched the silver baton. It didn't weigh a tenth as much as the chisel he'd once lugged up the basement stairs, and even in his weakened condition he was able to take it easily into his mouth.

Squatting on the stool, the baton held lightly in his teeth, he cased the stage. In the wings musicians were smoking cigarettes and chatting and sipping from mugs. None of those who'd remained behind seemed to notice him. He hopped down off the stool and scooted stage right, back down the steps.

Before long, the stage filled up with musicians again. The last two people to return were the conductor and the one Toes had identified as Sebastian's cousin, Thaddeus. Thaddeus sat in the concertmaster's chair while the conductor perched on her stool again.

"Very funny," the conductor said, her voice rising above the tuning of instruments. "But aren't we a little old for this sort of thing?"

The musicians all gave her blank looks.

"My baton," she said. "Who hid it?"

The musicians exchanged glances, but no one said a word.

"Really," the conductor said, becoming a little exasperated. "Now we're wasting time."

"Come on, people," Thaddeus said, rising to his feet. "April Fool's Day was months ago."

"Thad, look!" cried a pretty blond woman. "Up there."

Everyone looked where she was pointing her slender silver instrument: up the concert hall's center aisle. Near the doorway to the lobby sat a black cat with the silver baton in his mouth.

Toes just looked from the pretty blond woman, who bore a strong resemblance to the one in the long-gone photo on Sebastian's night table, to the conductor.

"Well, for heaven's sake," the conductor said, hopping off her stool. "Stand in for me, Thad, will you? I'll be right back."

She strode across to the right side of the stage and down the short flight of steps. When she was halfway up the center aisle, Toes turned and scurried out across the lobby. The last thing he heard as he left Philharmonic Hall was the musicians' chorus of amused laughter.

Toes padded down the grand front steps to the sidewalk, where he turned around and watched the conductor stride out onto the sunny portico.

"Please, cat, stay right there."

She had a kind voice and an amiable face, but Toes couldn't obey her. As soon as she was halfway down the steps, he took off down the sidewalk.

"Cat, please!"

Toes stopped. But once she started down the sidewalk, he set off again. At the first intersection he scampered across, mounting the opposite curb just as the DON'T WALK sign started flashing. He looked back. The conductor just missed the light, giving him a chance to catch his breath.

It went on like that for four blocks. On the fifth, Toes had to duck under a parked car to avoid a postman wheeling his mailbag along, and on the next block he was confronted by an even more alarming sight: a boy dribbling a basketball, pounding it murderously against the sidewalk. Toes peered over his shoulder. The conductor was only about ten yards behind him, her face flushed from trying to run in a rather tight black skirt.

Fate smiled on Toes again. There was a rare break in the flow of traffic out on the avenue.

By the time he pulled himself up onto the median strip, he had to spit out the baton and pant for breath. If the conductor had dashed right after him, he would have been caught. But she'd missed her chance. And by the time there was another break in the traffic, he'd recovered.

When he finally got home, Toes waited under the front step till the woman arrived.

"Please, cat," she pleaded. "This is crazy. Just let me have it."

As she bent down to grab the baton, Toes darted into the narrow passageway. At the end of it he looked back and saw the woman following, stepping carefully as she negotiated the puddles and litter.

When Toes emerged into the little backyard, he was relieved to hear Beethoven pouring out the open window. Minerva was still perched on the outer sill. Judging by the astonished look she gave him, she must not have seen him slip out of the house earlier. He dropped the baton in the weeds and circled behind the rusty table.

As the conductor stepped into the backyard, she blinked her eyes. "Thank goodness," she murmured, noticing a glint of silver near her feet.

As she stooped to retrieve her baton, Toes slunk around behind her and scooted off down the damp passageway.

12

For a moment the relieved conductor just stood there waving her precious baton along with the Beethoven. But she was keeping the whole orchestra waiting. She had to get back to the rehearsal.

Nevertheless, she stopped halfway back down the damp passageway. She'd assumed the Beethoven was a recording—it had even crossed her mind that it was by the late, great Yehudi Menuhin—but it suddenly struck her that this was impossible. It was the third movement of the Beethoven Violin Concerto: the Rondo. Yet after the soaring violin solo, the orchestra hadn't joined in.

She returned to the small, weedy backyard. She wasn't hearing things: there was definitely no orchestral part. It was only the violin. To the best of her knowledge, no one ever recorded the violin part alone.

Moving behind the rusty table, she made out the gleam of a violin in the open window, and a vigorously bouncing bow. Her heartbeat, just calming down after all her exertion, sped up again. Never in her life had she heard the violin part played so ravishingly.

When the Rondo ended, she approached the window. An explosion of wings startled her. She'd been so entranced by the music, she hadn't noticed a bird perched on the sill. As she watched the bird flutter over the roof, a voice came from inside:

"Minerva?"

"No, I'm afraid it's Maria. I hope you'll forgive me for invading your privacy."

The sash squeaked all the way up and a young man's face appeared: unshaven but not unpleasant.

"Minerva's a dove," he said.

"I'm sorry I spooked her."

"May I ask what you're doing here?"

"Trespassing, I suppose. It's the silliest thing in the world. A cat stole my baton"—the conductor held it up—"and I finally found it here. I'm Maria DeSilvero."

"So you are. How are things going with the Philharmonic?"

"It's a wonderful challenge. May I ask whom you play with?"

"I don't play with anybody."

"You're joking."

He shook his head.

"But . . . may I ask your name?"

"Sebastian Crabbe."

"Are you any relation to Thaddeus Crabbe?"

"Cousin."

"Well, Mr. Crabbe, you have the richest sound I've ever heard. And I've heard a lot of fiddling."

"Why, thank you," Sebastian said, his dark eyes widening. "I appreciate that."

"Would you consider doing some guest appearances with us?"

"Guest appearances?"

"Our fall season's set, of course, but one of the advantages of being conductor is you can fiddle with the schedule."

"Fiddle," Sebastian said, smiling.

"It would be an honor to have you play with us. In fact, I've been dying to put the Beethoven on the program, but it's so hard to find a violinist to do it justice."

"What about Thad?"

"Oh, Thad's wonderful. Technically, as sound as they come. But for that you need . . . inspiration. Let's see, I'm going away for the weekend, and next Tuesday we're leaving on tour for the rest of August. Could you possibly come in to see me on Monday?"

"But you've only heard me play once."

Her eyes flicked skyward. "I only saw that dove fly once, but I know she can fly. Shall we say Monday at eleven A.M. at Philharmonic Hall? It would be good to hear how you sound with the orchestra."

She held out her hand. Sebastian reached out and shook it.

"Amazing," she said. "It's almost as if that cat wanted me to hear you. Have a nice weekend, Mr. Crabbe."

"Please, come through the house," Sebastian said. "Would you like a drink or something?"

"No, I'll just cut through here. I was in the middle of rehearsal."

Before Sebastian could get to the back door, Maria DeSilvero had disappeared down the passageway. Sebastian went to the front door and opened it just in time to see her climb into a cab.

Watching it drive away, Sebastian wondered if he was dreaming. The new conductor of the Philharmonic had just stumbled into his backyard and heard him play. How likely was that? And heard him play one of the most challenging pieces in the repertory.

A cat had stolen her baton and led her here.

Sebastian shut the door and strode into the living room and lifted the afghan off the easy chair.

"Toes? Where are you?"

He went back into the kitchen. Toes hadn't touched his food since breakfast. Sebastian checked the basement: the little bathroom, behind the hot-water heater. No Toes. He hustled back upstairs and out into the backyard.

"Toes? Where are you, boy?"

But of course Toes wasn't a boy anymore. According to the vet, he was an old man.

The little backyard dimmed as a cloud crept over the sinking sun.

13

Of the many different kinds of TV programs Toes had watched over the years, his very favorites were the nature shows. He particularly liked ones set in Africa and Asia about noble cats like lions and tigers and cheetahs. But the most memorable nature show he'd ever seen hadn't featured cats at all, only elephants. Hulking and homely as the creatures were, Toes had admired them greatly, especially the way the parents protected the young and the way the elderly ones trooped off to die in a hidden, private place. They made him think of his mother.

The last thing he wanted was for Sebastian

to find his corpse and get depressed, but unfortunately Toes didn't know any hidden, private places to die in. So after leading the conductor to the backyard, he scurried out onto the sidewalk and headed the opposite way from earlier: out of town, instead of toward the city center. Perhaps he could find a hidden, private place in the countryside.

As he trudged along, block after block, the neighborhood became greener and more suburban, but it was a hot summer day, and well before he reached any countryside, a wave of fatigue crashed over him. He collapsed on a strip of grass between a curb and a sidewalk. The trunk of a little tree shading him had clearly been marked by a dog, but even so Toes couldn't go another step. He couldn't keep his eyes open. If the dog was nearby, he was a goner.

But the dog must not have been around. Nothing bothered Toes till eventually a fly started buzzing around his snout. Soon a couple of the flies' comrades arrived and joined the fun. Faintly aware of their buzzing,

Toes thought of another nature show he'd seen, one in which a slain zebra had been so covered with flies that you couldn't even make out the white stripes.

A sudden breeze blew the flies away. Or was it a breeze? Conscious of an odd, fluttering sound, Toes made an effort and opened his eyes a crack. There, perched on the grass beside him, was Minerva, flapping her wings.

Toes was so astounded, he forgot how weary he was.

"Minerva?" he said, lifting his head. "What are you doing here?"

Minerva stopped flapping and cocked her head to one side, aiming one of her gentle eyes at him.

"Why aren't you home with Sebastian?"

Still Minerva made no reply. But off to his left, Toes heard a squeaky tittering. He swiveled his head and saw a pair of mice perched by the grate to a storm sewer under the curb.

"What's so amusing?" Toes asked.

"You," said one.

"Coo," said the other.

"What?" said Toes.

"Coo, coo, coo," said the first mouse. "It's all doves know how to do."

As a moving van came lumbering down the street, the two mice dove down into the storm drain.

Toes turned his head. There was Minerva, still beating her wings to keep the flies off him, so close that even in his weakened state he could have grabbed her.

"You can't talk?" Toes said.

Minerva cooed.

"You mean, all these years I thought you were ignoring me and . . ."

Minerva cooed again.

"So when you saved me from the snake, that was . . . Gosh, I'm such an idiot." The thought of all the time they'd spent together listening to Sebastian play made Toes want to give the bird a hug. But of course that would scare her to death. So he just said: "I hope you won't think too poorly of me when I'm gone."

Minerva cooed softly and sweetly. Toes was

so touched that he actually felt stronger.

"You're a true friend, watching over me like this," he said. "If only I knew . . ." He turned his head. "You know, there's something . . ."

There was a flagpole across the street, with no flag flying, and under it a bike rack empty of bikes. An ancient memory swam up out of the depths of Toes's mind. It was the school where John McDonahue had exhibited him to his science club.

"You know, Minerva, I once asked you if you'd ever seen a backyard with a white stake between two bushes. I know you can't answer, but if you've seen anything of that nature, could you show me the way?"

Minerva flew straight up into the tree. As soon as Toes struggled to his feet, she flew down the street and landed in another tree. Toes dragged himself after her.

It turned out that the house of his birth was only a few short blocks away. The McDonahues had replaced their dark-blue SUV with a silver one, but he would have recognized the house anywhere. The sprinkler was even going in the front yard.

He limped around to the back of the house next door and, skirting a ragged vegetable garden, found the compost heap where he'd landed years ago. He could no more have climbed the towering stockade fence today than he could have played Sebastian's violin, but after nosing along the base of the fence, he located a place where one of the wooden slats had rotten out. Squeezing through, he found himself under a yew bush. He crawled out from under it. His vision was blurring, but across a corner of lawn he could make out a pair of bushes.

He dragged himself over to a white marker between them. As he tried to make out the faded writing on it, the stake multiplied. He shut his eyes and slowly reopened them to clear his vision. But no. He still saw multiple stakes: not one but four.

He walked toward one of the imaginary stakes—and bumped his head. It was real. What's more, the writing on this one hadn't faded. He couldn't decipher the word, but underneath the letters were numbers, and thanks to all the sports he'd watched in his kittenhood, he was pretty good at numbers. There were two dates: the year of his own birth followed by the year five years later. He checked the other new stakes. Each had a different word at the top, but the numbers were all identical.

He dragged himself back to the first stake and curled up beside it, utterly worn out. His eyes drooped shut, his snout dropped to the ground, and he drifted off on a memory of how warm and safe he'd felt as a newborn, before he could open his eyes, being stroked and bathed by his mother's tongue.

Suddenly he couldn't breathe—and for a terrible moment he was buried in the litter box again. His head jerked up; his eyes jerked open. Instead of the leering faces of his siblings, there were only the white stakes, but even so he was trembling all over.

He heard a coo, soft and long drawn, and blinked up at a fuzzy shape perched atop the stockade fence. Minerva was still watching over him. The loyal dove cooed again, a pitch-perfect A, and gradually Toes began to hear Sebastian's heavenly violin. The notes soared and swooped, saddening and gladdening, and little by little Toes's trembling ceased. In his mind he heard the simple Bach air Sebastian liked to save for last. Closing his eyes, he meowed a little variation. He even composed a mouse lyric in his head.

At first I was so warm,
But now I am so cold;
At first I was so young,
But now I am so old.

His meowing was so feeble that not even Minerva could have heard him. But Toes heard, and in spite of the chill creeping over him, he glowed inside to think that he, a mere cat, had finally made a little music.

14

For the life of him Sebastian couldn't figure out how Toes had jumped out the window while he was playing. He'd been wrapped up in Beethoven, certainly—but the window was right at his elbow. And wouldn't Toes leaping out have flustered Minerva even more than Maria DeSilvero had? Yet that was the only open window in the house. And Toes *must* have been the cat who'd stolen the conductor's baton and led her to his backyard. What other cat in the world would—or could—perform such a feat? And now, after pulling off this wonder, Toes had vanished into thin air, leaving Sebastian no one to thank, no one to share his jubilation with. It was almost as frustrating as it was miraculous.

After searching every corner of the house and backyard, Sebastian scoured the neighborhood, walking blocks in every direction, calling out "Toes!" over and over. But the only response he got was from a man who leaned out the window of an apartment building and yelled, "Hey, can it, buddy, will ya?"

When the daylight started to peter out, Sebastian returned home, got into his car, and made a wider tour of the city. The darker it grew, the more unlikely it seemed that he would be able to spot a black cat, so he finally drove home and called the police. The desk sergeant at the local precinct house was courteous, but it didn't sound as if he was going to make a missing cat one of the force's top priorities.

Without Toes curled up on the foot of his bed, Sebastian didn't sleep very well. He got up early the next morning and searched the neighborhood again. Things were quiet, since it was Saturday, and at one point he heard a cat yowl from behind a Dumpster by a construction site.

But all he found there was a couple of scruffy alley cats.

At lunchtime he went home and drew a picture of Toes on a sheet of paper. Below it he wrote in black Magic Marker:

Missing black cat
Highly intelligent
Name: Toes (on collar)
Kind of skinny
Seven toes on each paw
$500 reward

He wrote his phone number at the bottom of the sheet and drove to the copy shop and made a hundred copies. He posted them on telephone poles and phone booths and bus shelters all over that part of the city.

After another fitful night's sleep, Sebastian woke up to a mockingly beautiful Sunday morning. He opened the back door and all the windows so Toes could get in if he came home. Then he sat slumped at his desk, staring at the phone. As the long summer day

MISSING BLACK CAT
HIGHLY INTELLIGENT
NAME: TOES (ON COLLAR)
KIND OF SKINNY
SEVEN TOES ON EACH PAW
$500 REWARD

dragged by without a call, he felt more and more disconsolate. Now and then he glanced over at the violin propped up on the chair by the open window, knowing he should be practicing for his appointment with the Philharmonic the next day, but he just didn't have the heart to play without Toes around to listen. He was feeling sorry for himself, he knew—but he couldn't help it. Even Minerva had abandoned him.

15

Minerva was perched atop the stockade fence at the end of the McDonahues' backyard. She'd been there for the last two days, keeping a watch over Toes. Midway through that afternoon she flew down and shooed some flies off him with her wings, but this time he didn't open his eyes and talk to her.

Not far away, inside the McDonahues' house, Mrs. McDonahue was poking her head into the TV room, where Mr. McDonahue was watching the final round of a golf tournament.

"Let's have a cookout," she said. "I got a nice London broil."

"Great," said Mr. McDonahue. "Tell Tucker to set up the grill."

"Tucker's over at Mikey's."

"Tell Melissa then."

"She's at the mall." Melissa was now sixteen.

Mr. McDonahue sighed. What with John off living with college friends, that left only him. So at the next commercial break, he set up the grill in the backyard, just getting back in time to see the tournament leader can a par-saving putt.

Soon the front door slammed as only Tucker could slam it. He didn't call out hello, simply clomped up the stairs, shut himself in his room, collapsed on his bed, put on his headphones, and cranked up the music. He was now fifteen.

At a little after six, Melissa got home, and though Mrs. McDonahue wasn't crazy about the skimpy top she'd spent her allowance on, she kept this to herself and managed to cajole Melissa into setting the picnic table. Soon she joined Melissa in the backyard, carrying out the marinating meat, and once the golf tournament was over, Mr. McDonahue came out and lit the coals. Only when the smell of sizzling meat wafted into Tucker's bedroom window did he deign to take off his earphones and come down.

But while Tucker was the last one out in the backyard, he was the first to spot the black cat curled up between the azalea bushes. He walked over and nudged it with a Nike.

"Hey! There's a dead cat over here."

The others quickly joined him.

"I'll be," Mr. McDonahue said. "Remember Toes? I think it's him."

"No way!" Tucker squatted down and inspected one of the stiffened cat's paws. "Hey, it is! Seven toes!"

"Good grief," Mrs. McDonahue said. "Where do you suppose he *was* all these years?"

"Maybe he came home to die," Melissa suggested.

"Imagine that," Mr. McDonahue said. "I always said he was smart. Do you kids remember John's box? How Toes figured out how to open it up?"

"Yeah, and the others were clueless," Melissa said.

"He outlived them all by two years," Mrs. McDonahue said, glancing at the outlying stakes.

"I guess the poor old fellow wanted to be buried by his mother," Mr. McDonahue said. "Get the shovel, will you, Tucker?"

"Hey, look at this," Tucker said, detaching a ring from the cat's collar. "There's something besides his name tag."

He stood and held up the ring. Alongside the brass name tag was a shiny medal.

"That looks like gold!" Melissa cried. "Let me see it!"

As Tucker jerked his hand back, the ring flew out and landed on the grass about six feet away. The two kids scrambled after it but lost out to a bird who swooped down, hooked the ring in her beak, and rose up into the air.

The four McDonahues stood gawking as the bird, a pearl-gray dove, soared over the roof of their house and flew off into the sunset with her prize.

Sebastian was sitting at the kitchen table staring glumly at the window over the sink. The daylight was dying out and there still hadn't been any response to his missing-cat posters. He knew it was silly to get so worked up over a missing animal, but he couldn't help himself. The darker it grew, the worse he felt.

Eventually he went into the other room and flipped on the TV for company. But it only made him think of Toes. He turned it off and shuffled back into the kitchen. Flicking on the light, he saw that the leftover filet mignon on the plate on the floor had attracted bugs. He took it out back and scraped it into the garbage can, then went back inside and cooked the other steak, hoping the smell would attract his friend. He cut the meat into morsels and divided them into two dishes. One he set on the kitchen floor, the other in the backyard.

He sat at the rusty outdoor table in the dark listening for a meow until rap music blaring from one of the housing projects drove him inside. Even then he left the back door and windows open for Toes. To drown out the noise, he put a Mahler symphony on the CD player.

He sat slumped at the kitchen table long after both the rap and the Mahler ended. He had no appetite for dinner. Finally, well after midnight, he locked the back door and headed for bed, but instead of sleeping, he tossed and turned, thinking of how Toes used to nudge his ankle to encourage him to practice; thinking of the thousands of evenings Toes had kept him company, eating with him, watching TV with him; thinking of Toes hiding his car keys the night he'd gotten drunk; thinking of

Toes mysteriously luring Maria DeSilvero to his backyard.

It was four A.M. before Sebastian finally conked out, and when he opened his eyes, the bedroom was full of sunlight. It was ten after ten! He jumped up and hustled into the kitchen. The filet mignon in the dish on the floor hadn't been touched. He unlocked the back door and threw it open. The food out there was gone.

"Toes?"

No reply. The food could have been eaten by mice or squirrels or rats or racoons.

There was no sign of Toes in the garage or the basement. In the living room a candy wrapper was perched on the couch, and a leaf was leaning against the computer keyboard, both presumably blown in the open window. But no Toes, not even under the afghan.

He wasn't under the bed, either. Sebastian trudged into the bathroom and, leaning heavily on the sink, checked his unshaven face in the medicine-cabinet mirror. If he hurried, he could still make his eleven-o'clock appointment at

Philharmonic Hall, so he took a quick shower, shaved, and put on his cleanest khakis and a blue oxford-cloth shirt and his least-scuffed shoes. But then he made the mistake of glancing at the foot of the bed.

Sinking down there, he stared into a little cave in the rumpled blanket. It was empty, and he felt exactly the same.

He had no idea how long he'd been sitting there when suddenly the phone rang, giving him a jolt of hope. He hurtled into the living room and picked up on the second ring. But it wasn't someone responding to one of the missing-cat posters. It was just old Mr. Kreisler from the music store.

"I vanted you to know ve finally got in that Haydn score you vanted," Mr. Kreisler said in his thick German accent.

"Oh" was all Sebastian could manage.

"I vill save it for you, Mr. Crabbe."

"Thanks," Sebastian said.

After hanging up, he shuffled back toward the bedroom but stopped short of the doorway. It might have been a trick of the light, but there seemed to be a strange glint on the violin propped up in his playing chair. He walked over and pulled what looked like a key ring off the A-string peg. Instead of keys, the ring held a familiar gold medal and a brass name tag.

In a small park a few blocks away stood a statue of a World War Two infantryman. Minerva had perched on the soldier's bronze shoulder many times, and though she was now perched just outside Sebastian's open window, the statue came into her mind as she peered in at her human friend. Had he turned into one, too? Ten minutes passed and he didn't so much as move a muscle. But unlike the soldier, who gazed off at the horizon, Sebastian's eyes were fixed on the medal and name tag in the palm of his hand. He didn't even move when the phone rang again.

On the fifth ring, he seemed to come to, and on the sixth, his eyes shifted to the phone. He lurched over to his desk and picked up the receiver.

"Hullo? . . . Oh, yes, Ms. DeSilvero. . . .

Yeah, I know. I'm sorry. Something happened. . . ." Even as he spoke into the receiver, his eyes remained on the glimmering things in his hand. "In an hour? Twelve-thirty? Um, that's really nice of you, but . . ."

Minerva watched his eyes shift her way: or, perhaps, to his violin. Then they shifted to the afghan in the armchair. Then back to the violin. Then to the palm of his hand. As they flicked back to the afghan, she saw that his eyes were shiny.

Sebastian cleared his throat. "Thanks, Ms. DeSilvero. I'll be there."

As he hung up, Minerva let out a coo.

"Minerva," Sebastian said. He held up the ring. "Did you bring me this?"

She cooed.

"Is Toes . . . ? He's dead, isn't he?"

Minerva cooed. Sebastian lowered his eyes to the spot under the music stand where Toes used to sit while he played. He stared there so long that again Minerva wondered if he'd become a statue.

But he finally looked up and wiped a

sleeve across his eyes. "He was quite a cat, wasn't he?" he said softly.

Minerva cooed.

"Do you want to know something strange, Minerva? Today's August fifth. It would have been his seventh birthday." Sebastian ran a finger across the scroll on his violin. "Do you think that could mean something?"

Once more Minerva cooed: a perfect A.